The . Series 1

This Collection

These are a collection of letters I, Michael Hip, wrote to my ex and various other people. I have grown since the beginning of that relationship, but I have a lot more growing to do. Everything has happened for a reason.

And with the changing of the seasons, I plan to leave this behind. So why publish it with Sara and Chester publishing? Cause maybe, in between these lines, there's some lessons to learn. Maybe there's something to be taught here. And even though I'm relatively okay today, I'm still stuck in the illness maw.

I loved her, and I was infatuated with her. I wish I could have known she wasn't the same. I wish I could have seen the show. So as you read these poems, take something from it that I couldn't. The lesson I wouldn't acknowledge.

I saw The sparks of conflagration, but I ignored it as my skin burned. This first collection I call “Hesitation.”. It shows my hesitation for this relationship I entered. looking back, I wish I would have believed that feeling not as paranoia...

But as a warning.

Hesitant

Yours Truly. Mickeal

Uhm, Dear Leah,
Sorry I left you in the middle of this desert
My minds bringing the heat of the sahara
My inconsistent impatience hurt
Your Letter was left on my desk
It was quite modest
Opposite of burlesque
I don't know what I was to expect
It was written with the bottom of respect
Yet, I don't know why, I'm hesitant
Didn't mean to come of as resistant
It's just hard when faced with such acceptance
I apologize, yeah I'm better than that
I apologize, I'm better than that
It's like a cat in a hat
I was expecting it to claw me, but that is not fact
That's fiction
Is there a hidden meaning in your diction?
Sorry for all the riddlin'-

Even in my head, fears spiralin-
Mysteries got me filled up on your nectar
Sorry if this comes off as a lecture
Feel like a soldier
Facing this bold cold structure
You wrote me last week
And my response might be meek
I'm like a pipe leak
Drip drip drop
Can't make my mind stop
I wrote my name at the top
But honestly? It's hard to think you won't hop
Hip hop away
It's scary, and I can't tell if it's the idea that you might stay
Or that if I open up my arms, you'll run away
My mood swings, sways
A tree in the breeze
My feelings- I can't explain with ease
Sorry if this is cheesy
I'm the wind breaker to a breezy,
Winter morning
My ex, I'm mourning
I hope I'm not boring
Kinda yapping, and it's eleven in the morning

It's been a while, you've been holding like a soldier
I left you with a cold shoulder
I act childish. Act older
The world, these days, is a lot colder
Yes sir! I remember
It was the end of November
I came out, and in December
I was kicked out of the house forever
I turned my back on the girl
They want me to be
Saw The cold depravity of this world
The name on that certificate ain't me
And I built myself like a Jenga block
Built myself a name from the ground up
Sorry if this is really personal stuff
And knowing my luck
This won't be put in the blue mailbox
Waiting for some "just right" time, goldilocks
Waving through a river of rocks
Check that metaphor off my box
I'm not writing, I'm just running
My words are just gunning
Sorry if I am bumming

In a way, the more I write, the more it's numbing
It's just- that person in the mirror
Isn't making things any clearer
There's this fog, transitioning in the mirror
Long hair, cut down to its fiber rear
Scars on my chest
Muscle instead Of breast
I'm writing this cause I can't rest
Maybe- for you, I'm not the best
Ever since I left
I've never been the best
This, along with the rest
Is a warning, don't fret!
I understand if you wanna leave
I'm practically trauma dumping on my knees
I understand, believe me
But if you got a second more, listen, please
I'm not good at this writing thing
And I want more than a fling
Feel like I took too long, digital ping
I'm no peasant, no king
No jester, no merchant
Not even ancient
Somewhat cultured
Surviving among the vultures

The . Series 7

Are we black or white or grey lines?
Did you really mean it, you wanna be mine?
Yes it's the old rule, rare to be kind
Bitter is the taste of fear, watermelon rind
Maybe I should take a second
Hit rewind
Probably be for the betterment
Going beyond The staff, ledger lines
When I'm gone, what will they remember me as?
Sorry if this is a side tangent
Did I finally make a name for myself at last
Am I just the sum of my past?
You wrote me three or four times
I was so scared, I hid each time
I tried to find some meaning inbetween the lines
I was looking for gold in a coal mine
The missing puzzle piece
Love, that's what I need
Am I living the life I wanna lead?
Sorry if this is repetitious to read
I guess in short, I really love you
And the more I ignore it, I diss you
And the more I think, the more it's true
It's like staring at the vast ocean- so blue
Did I come off the same?

Did I sour my name?
It's preferred, probably
But is it a game?
Or am I questioning reality?
Sorry that it took so long to hit you back
You came after the downpours aftermath
Who's getting the last laugh?
If this was a song, would I be considered a backing track?
And as I sit here in my dorm, man
I think about when you touched me with those smooth hands
Lady Liberty should look at you as a replacement
We were at the bar, drunk land
You wrote me, one week after
Then another
Again, another
And now I'm responding to your letter
What does that say about my character?
If this letter could be described, it's a fracture
Cause I can't stay together
Ignoring all literary structure
Hope I don't alert you
Didn't mean to desert you
Sorry if my silence hurt you

I wanna make it work, true
And you said the same
Similar, we had been played
A narcissists game
That much, you laid,
Down on the table
In a way, this is a fable
There's some sort of central idea
In this mess of cables
And as I look out the window
Into the world, it looks less hollow
Wanna get some coffee tomorrow?
Sorry if this filled you with sorrow
Did I do that?
Please, peer review, only the facts
Back to those gray lines, retract
There's no guarantee, that's the fact
That you will even hit me back...
But hey, if you do
I'll be waiting, sailing in those eyes of ocean blue
Entangled in those brown vines of you
And I'll be that person who
Couldn't amount to the same as you
I was stuck in this vacuum
And as I continue

Things are getting a lot calmer
Did I make this a lot harder?
I need an ice tea- Arnold Palmer
Hey, I heard tomorrow's suppose to warm
Finally, something positive
I have a habit to focus on the negative
But that wasn't my prerogative
I guess the wind just had a directive
Try to look at it from my perspective
Your status, in respective
I took so long to write this, opposite
Of- sorry for the imagery- laxative
Do I apologize too much?
Am I a coward?
I love you, and I miss you
Both of those lines are true
Storms passing overhead
The last of us been living as the walking dead
Took one shot of lead
To get some common sense in our heads
Do you ever feel the same?
I mean your cis, right?
So you kept your name
Am I right?
And as this letter runs on

I see this as no option
Sorry for the talkin'
If I'm being honest. Your profile, I'm stalking
If that's creepy let me know
Just wanted to make sure you're who you show
Even I admit, it's kinda low
Been planting these seeds in the sow
Hope you can understand the toil
A seeds only as good as it's soil
Only sprouts when watered and boiled
If I'm being honest, maybe I'm loyal
Is it weird that in my eyes, you're royal?
This is heating up to a broil
Did I say my name? I'm Mickeal
English major if you haven't guessed
If this was a class, did I bomb the test?
I was honest
I tried my best
Isn't that what you asked?
To quote your holy text
"Be your honest self, that's the best
That's who I picked out of the rest
There's no bombing this test
Really, just do your best"
Did I do that?

Or did I overlook that fact
Back to that
Sorry I never hit you back
Hope this pays you back

To
Leah Johnson

Ocean

Your's Truly, Mickeal

I sent out the letter
Feel like I should write another letter
I picked up the needle, ready for the stitch
Hope it got to you with no hitch
But I already know the answer
Before me on the desk is the letter
Just one, signed "Dear lover
Sorry I sent you one after another
I understand, the feeling of going under
When I was six, I had no mother
Forget about my father
You're no bother
Just so you know, we gotta look out for one another
And I'm just glad you wanna be my lover
Coffee sounds quite nice
Decaffeinated or ice
Good to see we have a similar life

I understand the strife
See you tomorrow"
So now I'm excited for morrow
I'm smiling, getting over the sorrow
Along as I can spend it with you
I'd travel the vast ocean, for you
Sorry if it's weird
The way I fell for you
Your letters on the bathroom counter
Shaving my beard
Smiling as I look at the signature
Left by you
A feeling so true
New revolution, call upon me like a coup
Sorry if I'm not extravagant, escargot
Snails pace, I know
Got me feeling not low
Put some beard oil in
Look out to the college lawn
Out my window, won't be long
It's happy, wish I had some fitting song
Hope you appreciate music
My playlist needs a remake, they could use it
If you could do that, I'd appreciate it
This feelings hard to take as an axiom, Fact

If my feelings where a council, I'd ask em
How do you feel? Ask em
Do we have the same values, stick to them?
Or turn your back on them?
I mean you wrote in your letter
That we're similar to one another
But now I'm second guessing
Maybe I should be more trusting
Get my clothes on
Looking at the clock, all the time that's gone
Look out to the dimly lit lawn
Facing my beast at the maw
Thought this world was hateful, seemed like law
Still sorry I didn't write ya
I'm fifteen minutes late
For our coffee date
The sun is rising, this feeling you create
I guess mood is what you make
out of the situation
My defenses swept with persuasion
I walk on down to my car
I know the cafe isn't to far
Been stuck in this mood jail, staring out the bars
I pull up to the spot, forgive my literary spar

And there you were, standing under the six A.M
sun
You waited, didn't run
We sat in the booth in the corner
You said, you wanna explore this Further
Frappuccino wasn't the only thing on your order
Remember that prison I mentioned? You cut
Through the structure
The concrete fell to the ground
You lowered me down
Turned the frown
Upside down
I looked at your eyes
The way they light reflected
I looked at your eyes
Guess we have the same perspective
Guess I'm still questioning your directive
For once, not dissociative
It's nice to know, your not fictive
You smile at me, welcoming
You talk to me, calming
Got me in your hand, palming
The balls in your court, pulling
Me into your arms
We walked back to my dorm, wrapped arms

Walked up to the door, wrapped arms
Smiling, I opened the door, long arms
If you were a tree
You'd be the opposite of shady
Trust me
That if it's meant to be
I would be more than happy
And now it's night time
Looking at this paper of lines
You're sleeping on my couch
So lucky our dates entwined
I write this as a thank you
That much, I hope is true
I write this cause I love you
You feel the same, That's true
And as the clock ticks away
I'm glad I crossed your way
Remember when we met in class?
Only a month has passed
If you had asked me yesterday
On my dresser, your letter laid
Looking at that stamp
What did you pay?
Well, It's not the stamp you set out to buy
but the respect from this guy

The fool, head over heels
Kinda funny, How I feel
When I left, I gave up heels
And now, I know this to be real
Writing this with a rose in my mouth
And this love in my veins
Writing all the things my mouth
Will never say, aye
You rolled over onto the floor
I picked you up, laid you back down
You were sound asleep
I left the door open
Rising, agent of leven
Honestly, a week ago, I was thinking of leaving
Leaving this world behind
Almost justified it in my mind
But there, you lay
So peaceful, angels at play
Are you mystical as fae?
Now it's one A.M
Does this show who I am?
I remember when we held hands
Like a collab between bands
This album we write
It just feels so right

Still asleep
Little obsessed, your what I need
Am I what you need?
Let me know after you read
My heads getting tired
Need a little shut eye
But I keep writing
In you, I'm confiding
Cause everything I'm writing
Is because often I'm hiding
Behind grades and projects on my plate
Riding these feelings, noble steed
Grab a horse with a lead
Can't make a horse feed
Even if it's what it needs
But with you, I'll happily drink
Time keeps passing as I blink
Slippery, is this writing, skating rink
Feels like there's something here, hyperlink
Now it's morning, you're still sleeping
Month ago I was mourning, you're still sleeping
Little paranoid, you're still sleeping
So beautiful, is that creepy? Like a shadow, this feelings creeping
Onto the walls, into the college halls

It's Sunday, time for worshiping idols so tall
With heart, head and all
I trust you to make the call
If I'm what you want
Hope I'm not a lot
Writings how I talk
Should probably wrap this up
How do I wrap this up?
Didn't Sleep last night
I'm awake, no fight
Waiting for you to wake up
Cooking some eggs up
If I was a cat in a litter, I'd be a runt
If your a villian, I'll be the grunt
Give me the orders, I'll hunt
Still sleeping? Wake up!
I keep waiting, waiting
Contemplating, debating
Waiting. Again. Waiting
Wake up!
If your eyes are the sea, I'm wishing for a storm
You complete me, like a bosses final form
Finally this fantasy forms
Just trying to keep breakfast warm
Hey, sorry if I'm bombarding like a storm

I keep the oven starting, keep it warm
Some eggs bacon, getting cold I warn
You won't wake up-
I'm still writing sorry for the cheesy stuff
Hey, I love you
It's nighttime in the ocean blue
Seven O'clock, waiting for you
Eggs are getting cold, waiting for you
So peaceful, longing for you
Stretching, waiting for you
I look out the window, start of a new day
Middle of a sprinkling day in May
I thank you for your stay
You took me to the lighter shade of gray
I stepped outside for a smoke
Sorry if I'm acting like a bloke
You gave me a glimpse of hope
We're climbing mountains, you hold the rope
I'm just happy for your company
I'm just happy to accompany
And as I smoke with one hand
And write with a pen in the other hand
Onto the tiled walls of the halls
Your eggs on the table
Thanks for respecting my flaws

The . Series 22

This letter hopefully will be done on the table
I finished the cigarette, stamped it out
I guess this is what loves all about
I'm grateful
Quite thankfully
Not only for you
But the fact your reading this
And as I leave it for you on the table
With my name as a label
You wake up from your slumber
We're far away from how I felt December
And as you read this, I remember
The way you like your coffee after a slumber

To

Leah Johnson

Thanks For The Damage

With Spite, Mickeal

Dear parents, I'm writing cause your on my mind
As much as I try, I can't leave you behind
I guess in December you thought I'd crumble
under the pressure
Without a nuclear family structure, go figure
a cross on your fireplace, a smile on your face
Cause we exchanged words, a cold war arms race
Thought we were blasting off to some crisis
Sick of excusing your vices
Truthfully, you left me guessing
Everything you are, I'm besting
But hey, look inside the mirror
Maybe see that man you left in the rear view
Will you even see this letter?
Each line melding to one another
No, I don't think so!
Not because I didn't show

But because you disowned me
Said that I could never be
Forget your "daughter"
Left me for the wolves to slaughter
I used to keep my head down
Nod along with a frown
But these past weeks, have been so much better
It was me, right, the bother?
Taught my brothers I was their zister
If I could have kids, you'd be inspiration for me as a father
To be the opposite of everything you are
And honestly? That's not a low bar
But hey, Let's pretend God understands
And really meant it when you used your hands
To leave a permanent scar
Now I realize, I'm going Far
Farther than your consideration
Other than this, I believed in some fiction
When I got accepted into college, I wrote you
Said I loved you, I told you
Said there was room to forgive you
Never got a response from you
I guess you just can't admit it's a problem
So now I'm writing my own anthem

Thanks for the damage
Thanks for the lessons
Changing my skin like a salmon
This ocean is to vast in its expanse
To really let your inconsiderate mantra bother me
If God makes no mistakes, how could I be?
Asked you to get my a therapist
You said that would teach me liberalism
Hid behind your bigotry, your racism
Made me start cooking when I was twelve, preaching sexism
Said it was a "women's role"
That it was just "in my soul"
Feel like I've been treading on eggshells
Through Jesus's sandals
The son of God, now a justification for hatred
You're one of the church's wealthiest patron
Did you forget your neighbour's?
When your check became six figures
And now, I sit next of my girlfriend
She inspired me to wrap this loose end
Resent me, punish me
Have God strike me down, if that pleases y'all
Forget me, never forgive me

And as the spring rain falls
I'm starting to realize you've got a problem
Am I out of my mind?
Pumping up the heretic anthem
If your five five five
I guess I'm just sick-
Double sixes, conversion camp never fixes
Sexuality, it ain't persuasive
Always told me, I was better in the kitchen
I was the one you were hitting
If I could explain this letter- These words
I'm pushing into your skull, these words
Have been on my mind since December
When you took the Bible verses you conveniently remember
Hey, while you hate your neighbour's
Let's talk about that six figure wage
I've been working minimum wage
One of those "fast food slaves"
As you constantly said could be saved
Honestly, thank you, you saved
And additionally paid
My way to where I am today, hey!
Since we're talking about the past
Your excuses for your actions were half assed-

Now that we're taking a stab
Let's delve deeper
Suddenly the cliffs steeper
The one you threw me down
When you kicked me out of hick town!
But hey. It's just as Jesus said'
"Love thy neighbour
As long as he makes figures
And is white
And keeps his grip on his wife tight"
You know what, I could have summarized this
With two simple words, fuck you
But unlike you
I actually understand the weight of words
But unlike you
I'm better than using those words
Really, you're not my problem
Really, there's a lesson
In your selfish beliefs
The cost of your ignorance was steep
Despite your financial situation
I'm still paying for your ignorant fiction
I extended two olive branches
But you burnt those bio bridges
Your silence was louder than your words

The absence of any though, and afterwards
I blamed myself for your wretchedness
In a way I'm sorry for that, let's talk Jesus
He was a carpenter
Who wanted us to love one another
Died on the cross
Because the regime didn't like how he came across
Sounds familiar?
That situations very similar
You didn't like my life choices
Heard it with your whispered voices
Tried to hide your hatred at first
But then you realized this wasn't a thirst
It wouldn't go away, didn't like my lifestyle
Treated me like some animal in the wild
Your regime is vile
Honestly? If I was crucified
I'd still be more than you ever are or were
I might be financially poor
But I'm rich
And I actually respect my partner
Unlike your "Bitch"
I'm taking the needle, making a stitch
Hope this is metabolic, done tying slip knots

Always waiting for you to not-
Well- not be you
Never met someone who was like you
Because I understood and took to heart
What Jesus really should meant to you
And I know mom won't see this
I fill this abyss you left
With this poetic attack
Tying up the loose slack
All these words, tied together like a cigarette pack
Chain smoking each line back to back
Don't bother to write me back
J don't care about that, no
I'm done expecting you to show
Hey, I graduate in twenty twenty seven
This boiling point levels
I know you won't be there
If You had a funeral, I wouldn't be there
Guess that makes us even
No more dad, you're just Steven
Adam and Eve, your favorite reference
Who cares if it's Adam and Steve, No difference
I'll keep living my life
Separating yours from mine
There's no escaping now

Tired of asking how
Done taking a bow
Moving on now-
It's not my problem, it's not my fault
That's really what this is about
I was always some sort of property to you
This scars you can't undo
Done always waiting for you
This is like the moons orbit, coming back around
You planted the seed in depleted ground
A seeds only as good as it's ground
And I'm done living off your scraps
Done with it all, close to a wrap
But I got one more thing on my mind
Something I can't leave behind
Did you ever love me?
Can those brothers be what it couldn't be?
There's no guarantee
That you will ever read
These lines I write with a doctrine
Meticulously solderin'
This words like steel spikes
Grab my fangs- add some snake spite
And as you sit back on your recliner
While making fun of mother

Popping a Bud Lite
The things I've been through, you'll never go through
In fact, your apart of that
Hope you could understand that
But I know you can't
And when I seal this envelope with cadence
I'll be leaving behind everything you left for me
Again, not my problem, not my fault
Because without you, I'm as happy as can be!
Hey! Finally I'm at peace
The missing puzzle piece
I'm holding to who I am
That's more then the spite in your hands
There's no escaping now
Don't wanna hear how
You'll justify,
Cause I realize
I don't need to accept it
Done feeling like i'm interruptin'
My dorm room may have a light bulb and window
But more lights coming through this promise that tomorrow
I won't be trying to fill this hole so hollow

Quite the opposite of sorrow
Guess I wrote this because I need the last laugh
And after that
I'll mail this out with fifty cents
For some "freedom" stamp
Your absence
Of common sense
Ain't my problem- don't act surprise
This was a problem you made rise
Keep pushing that bullshit
Keep yelling, flinging spit
The sun rises, I'm like the British empire
The way I'm conquering through this divide
You made an oath when you joined the church
I'm just surprised- no one knew you lied
And as I sit on my couch, I'm wrapping this up
I know I said that too many times- all this stuff
On my mind is coming out
It's a water balloon- I guess you're just collateral
If we're different, make it parallel
Because I want nothing to do with you
That much was true
But hey! I'm just some tranny
If your narcissism was acting, you'd get an emmy

And if your spite was a song, It'd be a heavy metal grammy
Tired of babysitting your ignorance like a granny
Closing thoughts- I know I said a lot
But I hope it sinks into your heart
And in part
Goodbye, so long
Passing you by

To

Steve Hip

Washing Machines

Your's Truly, Mickeal

Hey, thought I'd write you back
Thanks For your help with that
Disownment letter, moving after that
Sitting here in the campus laundromat
Watching these machines tumble
Throwing you a catch, hopefully I don't fumble
I guess we'll have to wait and see how the cookie crumbles
That date was pretty good
I was thinking- a walk in the woods?
I know you're busy- nose deep in your textbooks
Thanks for all your help
Really, it's heartfelt
The rain beating on the window, leaving a welt
With the way it pelts, pelts, pelts
Your probably studying right now
I'm just wondering how-
I was so lucky to be your sow
Now that we're growing together. Let it Show

I'll be at your side
Whether rain or tide
I'll be here
And As my laundry goes around and around, in its soapy ride
I have some questions
Hopefully I'm taking facts, not fictions
If I'm being honest, I'm still hesitant
Not trying to be resistant
But this voice is persistent
Thank you for welcoming me in-
Thank you for taking me in
A freshman to a freshwoman
If I fall from this high, where am I landing?
After all my doubt, I have to ask, "Are you still standing?
Do you really take my words with understanding?"
It takes a woman to make a great man, manning
This fate we create, I'm not damning
This destiny, trying to fully realize this reality
Family isn't dictated by bloodlines, honestly?
I'm just glad to exist in the same reality
That you do, to see those pictures you post. Thats me

Standing next of such a beauty
Am I too much?
A sob story and such?
I'm not trying to rush
Honestly, I wish this paranoia would hush!
The more I think of you, the more I blush
Am I just obsessed?
I feel possessed
My minds in orbit, like this spin cycle
It's been like this for a short while
Typically I'd smoke, mobster style
But that addictions hanging from a rope, add it
To the pile
Of things I put in the back of my mind
Composting my words like watermelon rind
bitter was the taste
But now I'm making sure the fruit doesn't go to
waste
Hope I'm not a broken record, copy paste
But if I was, I admit, I have some scratches
Been opening doors and hatches
Been opening opportunity and latches
Letting go of all those twenty two caches
Does your love come with a price?
Or do you believe in charity

Is it like this washer machine
Where there's options in your variety
But your prices still have to be paid
Are you just in it to "get laid"
Am I just a trophy or status
Like a discord status
Am I just another class and grade?
Digging my grave with a spade
Will I be erased tomorrow?
Like a discord status?
Lost in your hips persuasion
Last night, you slept in my bed
I tried to sleep comfortably with your conviction
But I guess there's just that thought in my head
Wait a second, gotta unload the laundry
Wait, Ten Commandments
Not gonna pull any level of adultery?
Wait, someone of such accomplishments
To be slumming it with a transvestite
I overheard your mom on the phone
You guys didn't fight
She didn't leave you all on your own
Is that how it's supposed to be? Right?
In a way I'm jealous
In the other way, I'm zealous

I'm waiting for something that might not existent
Sorry, but I'm persistent
I'm waiting, contemplating, debating,
Are you just a passing merchant
Sailing to my island
Only to leave for richer lands
I'm not rich, far from it
Not lazy, far from it
Not wrathful, far from it
Just a bit worried- that's it
Not about if I can do the commitment
But more if I have enough accomplishments
To amount to you
We settled in an island, around us is the ocean blue
I wanna be with you, but in the same breath
I wanna be you, but in that death
I lose what you came to me for, but in the same Breath
Would you still love me in that death?
What is it you want?
Again, this washing machine circulates around and around
Tethered with pipes to the ground
I assume that I don't cause you to frown

But I just want to know, is it me that you want around?
My laundries done
Two kids across from me, talking about guns
Everyone's worried about this and that
But honestly? I'm worried about none of that
Nihilistic
I look at the world
Pessimistic
It looks back at me
Menacing
It used to be
Lately
I've been looking inwards
Honestly?
Is this who you want?
The person looking at me through the reflection
In the glass door
I see a couple kids smoking, think about my former addiction
Then, I see that reflection in the hallway floors-
Is that person me?
I mean, I try to be
The most authentic me
But I wanna know if that's enough

The callings tough
Making a decision for myself
Used to be told what to do by someone else
Symptoms of how I was raised
Systems of control, prayed
Prayed and prayed
But the gay wouldn't go away
Prayed and prayed
But the breasts didn't go away
Prayed and prayed
But the comments didn't go away
Prayed and prayed
But God didn't do anything, did I disobey?
I told you that, you smiled and held my eyes
I say something more in those eyes
Confused at what I saw
But you kissed, maw to maw
If love was the law
I'd be an officer
If love was the law
I'd pull you over
Just to let you know I care
But I probably made that more then clear
Maybe I need to be humbled
Did the message come across how I want it

Another catch, did I fumble?
I guess I'll know how the cookie crumbles
When you bake up a response
Now I'm sitting in my dorm, watching out the window to the lawns fence
Hope to show you something you showed me
If I'm obsessed, tell me
The answers probably before me
But hey, humble me
Sometimes I get so consumed
My ideas just bloom
And get lost in a literary vacuum
Just lucky to be in the same continuum
A soon as I started to doubt, I heard someone yelling to me
I looked down and saw you, smiling
You were just there to say you love me
That smiley bubbly feeling infected me
At least I know you thought of me
Almost thinking of scrapping this
But you told me to be honest
So I hope this is modest
Trying To be honest
You know, as an English major
It's hard to not give a shoulder

Trying to hold like a boulder
I know it's spring, but I'm used to expression that are colder
I'll be standing by you
That much is true
Your taking over my life like a coup
That's okay-
I'm quite fond of you
Maybe I didn't write this for you
Maybe I wrote this for myself
Guess that's the name I should put backed bottom
If above all and nothing else
Hopefully I'm not creating false problems
Feel like a binary system
Two moods, swaying back n' forth
But here forth
I'll be honest to me, won't question
Stop making such a fiction
If it's a moment, I'll live in it
Guess this is just another letter for the collection
Hearing a knocking on the door
Is that you?
Feel chained to the floor
Is that you?
Another knock at the door

Obsessed with you
Looking in the mirror
Obsessed with you
Grab some hair jell and keep my mohawk
Stare myself in my brown eyes
Button up my suit, turn the lock
And there you are

To

Mickeal Hip

Mood Swing

Truthfully, Mickeal

The pendulum swung back
Guess I should have expected that
A high is only sustained off of the drugs fat
You proved to be real, that's a fact
I just- got into a funk
A cadence, a cascading sound, crust punk
Knowing my own luck
I'll lost track of the puck
In this huge game
Let me break it down
I opened my mail and saw a familiar name
My father had sent it back without a frown
Quite the opposite
Guess opening it was a depressant
He's still debating his ignorance
Crying that I'm just a girl with arrogance
I'm not pandering to please him
Nothing will ever get through to him
Nothing will ever fix him

I know he's broken
I put his letter on the counter
Didn't open it, thinking of a counter
I remembered the way he treated my mother
The way he always hounded her
And that made me think
I was so used to it, didn't even blink
It was worse when he had more to drink
Does he even know he pushed me to the brink?
I walked around the envelope
I know he packed some spite in the envelope
Opposite to the sweetness of a cantaloupe
A hunter aiming at an antelope
I walked around it real slow
Thought it might show
Some reason to open it, no
It stayed there, no
It spread its infection
Founded in my father's fiction
I walked up to it
I could imagine it's got spite in the spit
Used to seal the envelope
Back to that metaphor of a antelope
My father, never calculated
A buckshot in a shotgun

I mean, I should have predicted
What was in the letter, inspired by rum
Eventually curiosity took over
He never wrote back to me
That energy of a cold shoulder
And I had to stand strong as a boulder
I opened it, very slow
As if I was treading with caution
He wrote it, I know
I recognize the handwriting and diction
I counted how many times he brought up Jesus
Wonder if the son of christ is sleeping well
Mistaking the lessons of Jesus
As a reason to manufacture my own hell
I opened the letter
It was on attack after the other
No status check on my brother
They still probably see me as a sister
I hate to think about it, lying down
My thoughts pace around
Back and forth, as I'm tethered to the ground
These feelings are suffocating, will I drown?
Collapse beneath the weight
Is this the hand of fate
You told me to be honest

I guess I write this as repentance
Your coming by to see me
The queen, checking on her worker bee
I can't pretend I'm a king
I'm worried about this thing
Sparked by my father, conflagration
Demanded me, subtly in the literary suffocation
Seems this wasn't as easy as I thought, complication
I'm thinking of my next affirmative action
Including my thoughts and farewells
Do I scrape the bottom of the barrel?
Or diversify, are we equal?
Acting like I should write a dramatic sequel
Is that what he wants?
Me to be like the rest of the foolish cunts?
He's probably talking among
His churches hegemony, a cadence they dance along
If I'm a gray line, he's a black dot
In the letter, he called me a tranny thought
I'm scheming up a plot
But does he deserve the thought?
Does he deserve what I got?
That's the battery inside my head

It's either respond back
Or understand, what's dead is dead
No need to tenderize the meat fat
I packed up my meal
And should I care how he feels?
I took the cards, struck up a deal
And do I have to take his spiel?
As you walk in my dorm
You might questioned this fetal form
You asked me, you cared
"How are you, why are you there?"
You took a risk, you dared
I sat all the way in the corner, "come here"
I said in a weak voice
You made the conscious choice
Ain't it funny
How mood can jump like a bunny
The contents of the mood, runny
Never cooked evenly, lumpy
That's why I love you
Because you're- you
And although my mood may be down
I know you'll be around
So hey, should I write him back
So hey, do I take his attack

So hey, hey, open up the card pack
Hoping that I can stack up
Some sort of excuse
For his abuse
Nah- as you told me
Live and learn, live and let be
Nah- as you told me
Families share the same wavelength energy
They can keep pandering to their ideologies
I'll make my own societies
Create my own diversity
If trauma was a class, I'd make it a university
You hugged and held me
And that's how I knew
I belong to you
I guess the seed grew
I cried into your shoulder
I cried, and you said
"I was your little soldier"
I cried, and you said
"I Love you, I'll be here
Through each and every year"
As if you banished my fear
Sadness's sobbing soon became happy tears
As I hugged you tight

I got so consumed by the dark, blinding was your light
You let me into your being
I want to be the person your leading
You show me. Just in your effort and being
That's life with you. Is worth living
And as we sat down, on the ground
You patiently waited for the storm
To make its rounds
You took on a protective form
Together, as if we were white doves
We levitate, this balled we create
Rising to the heaven above
We levitate, nourishing this seed we make
And as the storm passed on our island
You stayed, and when I stopped at last
You grabbed some tissues, you kissed my neck
You told me, you showed me what I should expect
You hugged me, dignity and respect
You took all of my words and began to digest
You live to protect
I used to live like a pessimist
And time passed by
I was lost in those blue eyes
The sun sets

The house always wins in a bet
But is love what we're gambling
You fell asleep holding me
A queen protecting its worker bee
And here I was, still making honey
The night comes down, falling over me
And yet, I'm in heaven
Call me a heathen
But I see something for us in those eyes
Hope fills my mind
And as we tangle ourselves endlessly
I live for your caring energy
Enough rejecting what is meant to be
I am yours, I am me
My mood swung yet again
A cycle that never ends
Eternally divine
If I asked you, would you be mine?
Blurry Is the gray line
But like a book, we bind
Laying out our stories
And our histories
I glanced around the bare room
I thought about how the seed we planted bloomed
If you had asked me a week ago

I would have said we were doomed
Now I see that's false
The seeds alive with its own pulse
And now that your so close
I feel my heart slowing pulse
You are the garden
You are the heavens
And if we are heathens
Then we were destined to be treated
As such, that much
I should seen, a lotus grows from the muck
And as I close my eyes
Fading into the ocean
I realize
That maybe, for once, we were meant to be
If you're taking a bite, do you like the taste?
Will you savor and not let me go to waste?
Am I the same, copy and paste?
Am I running into this with too much haste?
And I know when awake
You'll still be here
Left in the wake
Of this symphony we hear
Contemplating
All we left

Complicating
These feelings I got
We can go back and forth as the pendulum
swings
But let's be real, my father, my family?
Doesn't know a goddamn thing
And as we finalize and feast off the energy
They don't need to be on our fling
It's twelve A.M
I started this at five P.M
I should fall asleep
Since your arms are where I need
To be
Truly, me

To
Leah Johnson

Levitation

Lovingly, Mickeal

I will lift you up, my love
Embedded into your veins and blood
As you aura engulfs me again
The path beneath us bends
As we start our levitation
When did you make the decision
To cross paths
To ignore my past
To make something that lasts
And can I ask the question?
Is this a facade of fiction?
Will you levitate where I can't see you?
Levitate, where I can't reach you
Levitate, I can't forget you
If you were to make that paranoid delusion true
Am I all you need?
Do I age like mead?
The life we lead
Does it have enough to lead
Us down a path-

Us down a path
Where my consideration matters
Constantly climbing ladders
Do you know, you're my blood
You give me life in this flood
And I am paranoid
Is this just another tabloid
Sensationalize me
Paralyze me
Terrorizing me
Is this wicked fantasy
Will you levitate where I can't reach you?
Your always looking beyond the skies blue
Am I enough For you?
That I question, will we be submerged?
What will emerge?
Am I enough for you
Sitting on my bed, you're at class
Am I yours at last
Entering your study
I don't know why I have so much pessimistic energy
Is this a fictional fantasy?
That we survive honestly?
And like you did for me

Will you let me be
Your structure
You soldier
And as the battle wages on
And time has gone
You come as quickly as you leave
Your studying, and I'm on my knees
Every time you leave
I face the sky and please
Let this imitates
A ballad we will create
A garden we fabricate
This seed pollinated
Passing on its kindness
You saw me my weakness
You faced me with acceptance
Without mandatory tolerance
I don't know why I am hesitant
We made shelter on our own island
I sailed for so long, searching through the oceans violent
Predicament
Will you levitate where my love doesn't matter
Will You levitate, unreachable by my literary ladders

Will you levitate, surpassing anything possible
with feathers
Will you surpass me, and read these letters?
I write from my heart
I play my role, a heavy part
Is this just role-playing? Larp?
Your a picture frame
Is that your aim?
You complete me, I'll refrain
And tell you, your the reason I remain
Obsession reaches its climax
I saw an old cigarette pack
Two months ago, I'd stack
The tobacco wrap
And smoke until my lungs gave
But that's the effect of the person you saved
Me
Energy
Synergy
Long lost family
Will you levitate, as I watch out the window
Will you be here tomorrow
Will you embrace my mood swings and sorrow
Do you feel the love in your marrow
As I do

Sprawling the ocean blue
The world seems so much more-
Like you
And everything around me
You make it so much easier to be
Levitate, even if it means you must leave me
Levitate, if you don't need me
I'm doubting this reality
I'm recognizing thematic symphony
Levitate, take me with you
Levitate, bring me with you
To the galaxy
Divulge this fantasy
I'm watching time tick tock
We share the same mailbox
The same door lock
The same room
We built our foundation out of rocks
And every step next to the door
I'm expecting something more
It echos off the floor
Expecting you to open the door
A story of perfect plays
A reality I have paid
And this foundation we laid

Both having survived two decades
Overcoming our histories
Families ancestry
Star crossed over centuries
If they ever met in the universes of probability
Bring me with you, as you rise above your station
Bring me with you, when you knock on the doors of heaven
Bring me with you, even if I'm a heathen
Bring me with you, it's your decision
Levitate, where I can see you
Levitate, where I can kiss you
Levitate, where I can protect you
Levitate, levitate, Bring me with you
And as the universe ends
Give it a reason to begin
Sustaining myself off of your nutrition
Just right- for me and my situation
And as I see you leave in the morning light
I see, you as my whole life
Maybe I'm obsessed
This feeling has got me possessed
You gave me a refined purpose
And that's why I write this, with the same kindness

You showed me
You showed me all I can be
And I don't question you staying out late
And I look forward to all of our dates
Staring at a silver plate
While I wait for you at our restaurant dates
Time ticks by, fifteen minutes
I don't care how you spin it
Your presence, I appreciate it
You wrap me in holy linen
And I know that even if it takes a bit to show
I know you won't go
You'll always be with me
And as you walk in, I levitate
This feeling, we duplicate
My mind, you placate
With you in hand, lets levitate
In you, is golden blood
A holiness of an arc in a flood
And standing like old wood
An oak tree, where death once stood
You make this possibly
And honestly
The happiest
I will ever be

Your body is angelic
And your soul is optimistic
Destroying my values, which were nihilistic
To say the worst
And now I can tell
You will remember
My cracking bones
This web we spin forever
The storm over our seas
Dissipated like swarming bees
Our island we built, serving our needs
And as we eat
Our words, intimate
Knowing if we fall upon our blades
And everything we made
And will ever make
Will serve to us
How this dinner date is served to us
And as you walk out my dorm door
You levitate evermore
A plane running off the floor
Everytime you leave, I'm wanting more
I can tell that
Obsession is the fact
My mind does a lap

As I will not collapse
As long as I know
You'all come back
As long as I know
I'm more than that
Tranny who you date
That tranny who you placate
I do wonder why your always late
But you have a lot on your plate
So like a bird, levitate
So like a plane, levitate
So like a God, levitate
So like all you are, levitate
Just don't leave me behind
Just- please don't leave me behind
Is this something you fabricate
Or is this something worthwhile to commemorate
Go, steady into the night sky, levitate
I'll wait for you, I'll wait right here
Steady, into the galaxy, levitate
I'm happy to know your just out There
And our peers may judge
But they didn't deal with the emotions flood
They can all play jury and judge
Get lost in their ignorant flood

Please, stay with me
Please
Please, be with me
Please
I need the attention
Like viewers retention
I know I'm desperate
But I need to know
You won't levitate
Without me
You won't levitate
Without Me
Levitate, with or without me
Levitate, don't forget me
Levitate, complete me
Levitate, levitate...
Levitate

To
Leah Johnson

The Maw Of Our Seed

Lovingly, Mickeal

Under the chandelier
Under the stain glass
I know you won't disappear
Lessons from my past
Is it a relationship I fear
Cause you take the shadow, and cast
Them far away from here
Am I worthy of something that will last?
Show me your maw
Show me the strength of the bones in your jaw
Show me the ravens caw
Show me the bark and bite, the hawks claw
This island we built
Your always leaving
I feel The guilt
Cause I'm always pleading
For you to stay with me
Stay with me
For you not to leave me

Don't leave me
We leave ourselves vulnerable
I used to think my heart was impenetrable
You wanted me vulnerable
But you staying, is unpredictable
You got me in those jaws
Locking our maws
A study of loves laws
You shut the ravens caws
I know it's selfish, but please don't go
We fabricate this show
And make the script as we go
With you, I feel the opposite of low
The stained glass illuminates
This ballad we complicate
As you leave once again
I can't pretend
That, once again
I'm hesitant in the end
A slight bit obsessed
A little bit perplexed
A feeling so complex
Holding up my world, atlas
Stuck in your maw
This seed we planted grows

Stuck in your perforated jaws
And who else knows
Where we will be
In the coming years
Where will we be
In the coming years?
Watching you with eyes of a razor
Locked on like a laser
Don't leave me here
I know it's selfish, attack wanna me here
I know you have class
But that's a duration
I can not wrote
Determination
Keeps me glued onto you
Obsessed with you
I love you
Or so It grew
On me, the soil we planted
It's plain To see, we planted
The seed that now sparks conflagration
Another complication
Caged in your belief
I'm not good at keeping this brief
I can't focus on school work

And I hope I'm not a jerk
Always waiting for you to orbit back around
With my palms on the ground
You sail away, ambitions days
Show me which way you sway
I'm in pain as you leave me
You tell me
I'm too attached
I'm too obsessed
Back to that
It's not a fact
I'm infatuated
I don't mean to complicate it
I was once hesitant
But now I see, I've given up all resistance
And as the sun fade into the distance
I know as I listen
That when we awake, you won't be here
Am I hopelessly romantic
This feeling's addictive
With you I'm manic
Without you, I panic
This Ballad we play on repeat
This pattern upon which we feast
Quantum in the least

The days seem to repeat
The sun rises and falls like me
And every morning, you sail into the sea
Leaving me
And I pretend that without you I can be
But I can't
I can't believe
That without you
I can be me
My grades falling and flailing
Every class I'm failing
This fall, I'm detailing
You intention, I'm stalking
This feeling so hulking
Sitting in statistics, stuck in your maw
You got me attached to your thumb
Writing my paper, stuck in your maw
You got me more then under your thumb
I would be lying if I said
I didn't love it
I would be lying if I said
That I would want anything above it
I found an apartment
With the welfare department
We can make a home

If that's something you can condone
Run far away from here
Knowing what I fear
You leaving me forever here
You say I'm paranoid
But this voice has persistently annoyed
My mind, paranoid
Aren't you?
I mean, everythings moved so fast
And this is what I had longed for
But you feel so distant
And this is what I longed for?
This battle wages, this war
That our souls bare
Do you feel the same?
Crushing under the weight of a name
Everything that I had wished for came with a price
I've only experienced this twice
And as you capture my life
And help me with my strife
I see now, as I saw when we first met
I'm trapped in your maw and gaze again
This seed we planted, I can't pretend
That I'm not scared it will die in the end

I ask you why you're out so late, and you're defensive
As if I said something offensive
Why were you so defensive?
Was I offensive?
Does your love have to be so distant
Every night, we're continuums apart
Like separate chambers of the human heart
A desolate painting of art
Show me why you're so hesitant in my heart?
In this play, I play my part
And we go back and forth
As you take your glass and drink
Telling me it's just hard work
And that your studying
And between my begging and pleading
I'm studying
Why you're always puttering
So far away
Leaving me in your way
If I'm the darkness of your day
Do you want me out of your way?
And as we argue
And get so close to saying adieu
You pull me back in

Reeling me so I'm not leaving
I'm noticing
There's a pattern in this complicating
relation, It's your decision
Do you want me or not?
Say it with conviction
Cause I'm trapped in your jaws
We rushed into this relationship
Am I a lover, a project or a patient
This bed, though holding you, feels empty
Why were we so impatient
And every morning, you leave me
With this suffocating feeling
Is this God's Dealing?
This empty feeling
I mean really?
Is saying I love you in your eyes a chore
Am I just a bore?
Waiting for something more
But there's nothing in store
In our fates
I try to have faith
But it's just so hard as it complicates
This musical we fabricate
This pattern we replicate

Forever more
I'll be left so desolate
Forevermore
Back to the stained glass, standing in this church
Praying to God to end this hurt
Am I someone you love or hate?
Or just a project to placate?
I'd ask you
As this seed grew
If you knew
That I'm feeling so blue
It's been so fast
Will this actually last
Or just a replication of my past?
This shadow we cast
Do you see me as you saw me when we first met?
I'm stuck in your maw again
Did you see the fire in the sunset
I'm stuck in your maw again
Was this something I should expect
I'm stuck in your maw again
With all do respect
Is this how it ends?
No, I can't let it end
Even if I have to pretend

I need you as much
As you need me and such
A cycle will repeat
Till the end of this literary feast
Are you the savior I long for
Are you expecting more
Will we even make it into a score
Or just four months more
Is there something else in store?
I'm trapped in your jaws again
But even then
That's if you let me in
Into your jaws again
Is it a burden
To say my name every now and then
Is it a burden
That you let me in?
Or maybe I just need to sleep
Maybe rest is all I need

To
Leah Johnson

Literary Weapons

Apologetically, Mickeal

I'm sorry that I said such things
I'm sorry, I do love you so
I'll forget those false things
And I know
There's something more
There's something in store
Something I cannot ignore
It's my fault, nevermore
Will I question you
Will I question you, as you walk out the door
Will I question you
As I'm waiting for something that's just
So much more
I'll stop arguin'
And keep on hopin'
Stop mopin'
Cast me out like Ms.Jackson
Bombs Like words hanging over us
I'm stepping forth as such
It hurts watching you walk out the door

But I expect, you don't want me anymore
Hesitant as I hit the floor
Is your love symbolic of a lock door
That I'll be trying to open forevermore
That I'll be pounding against the floor
You say it's an overreaction once more
Need respect? You got it
Need devotion? You got it
Need support? You got it
Your little soldier, don't forget it
As I ignore my needs once more
Between the carpet on the floor
And the tears falling to my maw
Quivering between the teeth in my jaw
I'm scared that when you leave
You won't come back around again
My baby's sailing off again
And happy with it, I pretend
But in the end
It's so painful to pretend
But you say it's in my head
That the past is dead
And this fiction I read
Will lead our blooming seed to death
I'm sorry if I'm clingy

This sensation is clinging
And with all this emotion I'm bringing
I'm an anchor pulling
You down
Down
Down to the ground
Flipping your smile upside down
This battle we replay again
Between blood and castles of wood
We rebuild again and again
Between bad and good
We equip our literary weapons
Forgettin'
All of this, as we succumb
To said weapons
I'm sorry for staining your soul
I'm sorry for spilling my soul
Onto the carpet floor
Where the remnants of my soul
Soak evermore
I left a note on the door
An apology
Hope I did everything and more
But this dissonant symphony
Has become my cacophony

Is there a reality
Outside you and me?
Need support? You got it
Sacrifice? You got it
A soldier, you got it
You got it, you forget it
You say I love you
When I'm about to leave you
It kills me slowly
When we argue
It feels disingenuous
A little fictitious
I'm submitting to its vicious
Grip, so venomous
And each night I go to sleep
With you next of me
You say I'm what you need
But then you disregard me
Are we old enough to know?
That this is a toxic show
Are we old enough?
To say goodbye after hello?
And you think I wanna feel like this?
I'm sorry for being an abyss
And you think I respect this?

And I'm sorry if it's infectious
I'm sorry if I'm not enough
I'm sorry, I'm not enough
I guess I just have to toughen up
Will I ever be enough?
The way that it was
This will never be what it once was
The way it was
I'm sorry, I'm not enough
And if I left forever, would you notice?
I'm sorry if this is depressive
And if I died, would you notice
Or would I still be begging in my grave
For you to say my name
My name
And I am so ready
To forgive You
If it means you'll be happy
Never forget you
As we stand between
These collapse walls
Tear off the bandage
Bouncing off these concrete walls
I'm trapped in your bandages
It will never be what it was

It will never be what it was
And I will never be the same
If it means you'll say my name
It was never what it was
Was it?
As we sit and say nothing
Love, was it?
Or was that a mask too?
And I'm broken
Was that a mask too?
I'm sorry, I'm broken
Maybe I'm misunderstanding
Trying to do some rebranding
All these feelings I'm handling
Our love, once kindling
Now burnt out and fading
My sense of self, fading
I'm apologizing
Apologizing
For everything I am
And will ever be
What we had
Died because of me
You want a carbon copy? You got that
And you want someone to save? You got that

And maybe I won't see till after the fact
After the countless arrows in my back
And I guess I didn't notice
That it was my fault
And I guess I'll never notice
Who's really at fault
Long winded apology
Always apologizing
But you never admit fault
Always redirecting
Well I'm sorry for hurting
I'm sorry for disturbing
I'm sorry it's not working
And as you leave in the morning, I'll be mourning
What we had
What it was
What we had
What it will never be what it was
I'm sorry for it all, I can't leave my bed
I'm practically dead
And you sat, it's all in my head
As I sink deeper into the bed
We are too young to say goodbye
But I can see it in those shifting eyes
That I will never be fully realized

The sow we sewed has now died
Can you believe
That it's only been four months
And the growth has reached a stunt
Praying for just a single feeling in your fingers
I can't bear it anymore
Praying to be something more in those fingers
I can't bear it anymore
I'm sorry, but I can't open the locked door
I'm sorry, I'm nothing more
Then a fool, collapsed on the floor
I'm sorry, I can't be anymore
I'm sorry for all of this
This will never be what it was
And I'm sorry for this
For always wishing it was what it once was
But I have to know, do you feel the same?
I'm too tired to even care if you say my name
And every day, We play this game
If I was a feeling in your head, would it be shame?
I am so ready, to die for you
And it's so scary
The idea of what I am to you
And I'm not happy

But I'll pretend for you
But I'll bend for you
I'll end for you
I'd do it all again, for you
I never meant to hurt you
I never meant to break you
I never meant to hurt you
And, I still love you
That's why I'm still waiting for you
Looking out to the ocean blue
Waiting here for you
It will never be the same
As what it was
I will never be the same
As I once was
The way that you where is dead now
And I'm still asking how?
A chore you must plow
Dead is our Sow
If you feel it, act it
If you feel it, spill it
All over the floor
Show me something more
I feel it, I hate it
I feel it, do I create it?

I can't be anything more
What's in store?
What it once was
Is what it will now, never be
What it once was
Is now in the past for us
And I believe your excuses
As all my reasonings are excuses
I'm crucified in your gaze, Jesus
All these months, countless
Days, feeling useless
What it once was
Is what it will never be
Again
What it once was
Is what it will never be
Again

To
Leah Johnson

Is It Really Me?

Longingly, Mickeal

The clock moves closer to the hour
The spring begins it's shower
Flowers rise with the earth's power
As the roads get louder
My loneliness stalks these halls
My feelings hide within the walls
Still waiting for you to want to call
Me by my name and all
I wanna be with you
I wanna love you
Will you let me?
Do you love me?
Longingly Mickeal
Lovingly Mickeal
The sun sets, and you walk in
Your eyes beckoning
Despite all the broken
Feelings I'm holding
I still wanna be with you

I still want to love you
Do you love me?
Will you let me?
Again, longingly Mickeal
Again, lovingly, Mickeal
And I'll wait till I collapse
And wait for the tide to collide
I started smoking again, a relapse
We're separated in the same house, apartheid
Still waiting for the right time
Your so cold and sour like a lime
But I'm addicted
So I'll keep Hopin'
That I'll have a taste
And if I do, I won't let it go to waste
Everything that I gave to you
Was once what you gave you me
You used to look at me lovingly
Do I deserve somebody who loves me?
Do I deserve someone so above me
I'm on thin ice, I'll be kicked out
You're so above Me
So what is this about?
The longing for something you are possibly not
The longing for something that is not

Will I ever have what you got
Or just be someone you forgot
Just another somebody
In your life story
Just somebody
In your history
I'm just history
Aren't I? A skeleton to bury
I'll wallop in my misery
As you thread the needle and heal the wounds
You inflicted, the ones I succumb to
And as you wait for something new
I'll be waiting right here, trying to be something
deserving of you
Tear me apart
Forget me and my heavy heart
Somethings between us, I feel it
Somethings between us, I fear it
This love, we hide it
I've begun to fear it
Am I even a fascination
Deserving of your reputation?
Hey, while I wait for you to be pulled my
gravitational
Our seed is burnt in conflagration

Go on, thread the needle
But is it really me?
Go on, thread the needle!
Is it really me
That made such a steep hill
Is it me
Who is making this a living hell
Is it really me after it's all said and done?
This story can not be undone
Fade with sundown
As you bury any lasting memory of me into the ground
I'm feeling so below now
Bury me twelve Feet in the ground
Is it really me who's the problem?
Am I really the weapon?
When you look at me, do you regret it
Do you hold the future in your mitts?
Throw a pitch and miss it?
Go on, forget me
I'll be another figure in history
Go on, regret me
Now I understand the mystery
You show up late because you debate
Every situation I complicate

Is it worth It?
To come home and placate
My feelings and sensation
Coursing of ruination
Thread the needle?
That's your decision
Stitch me up
But I'm still bleedin'
Will you ever let me in
Where did this coldness begin?
Do I deserve to be let in?
Longingly, Mickeal
Lovingly, Mickeal
Apologetically, Mickeal
Spitefully, Mickeal
Your more than infatuation
More than another obsession
I'll keep waiting
While you spend your time debating
Whether I am worth it or should be forsaken
Pick up the prices but I'm forever broken
This smoke I've been attempting
This heavy situation I'm holding
This smoke, I'm addicted
As it kills me slowly

But I'll wait here lovingly
It's killing me slowly
But I'll wait, obsessively
Your possessing me
You leading me to believe
That I give you no option
But to leave
Sorry for all the misery
I'm still longing
Sorry for the history
I'm longing
Always longing and waiting for you
To come back from the vast ocean blue
It wasn't just in your eyes, that much I realized
That was just a full disguise
I'm a fool, that's a rule
I'll keep holding you up like a mule
I'll be your weapon and tool
I'll fight your battles, as a longing fool
There's nothing left of me
That's the reality
College knew this reality
And gave up on me
So now I live in that apartment
Working for the grocery department

Hide me in heart's compartment
This seed is fully tarnish
Everything that we grew and furnished
As been torn down and famished
This is not the finest
This is now our existence
Futile Is the resistance
I can self medicate with depressants
I can drink till my existence
Feels bearable
Your an unknown variable
Changing with the seasons
Changing without reason
So go on and thread the needle
Sew me up again
Go on and thread the needle
I can not longer pretend
That we were meant for eachother
In this perilous end
And as we look at one another
The seed comes to its end
Stuck in your maw again
Waiting for the cycle to begin
Shedding the walls of our loved, menstruation
Cleansing me of all we created

This period of time, dilated
I should have predicted
Our feelings are not relative
Though you say my concerns are reflected
You keep telling me it's in my head
So go on, thread the needle
Sew up the doubt in my head
So go one, thread the needle
I'll as patient as a horse at a steeple
Come on, maybe we are different people
Not to try to belittle
But look at where we once were
And what we are now
We're miles away from there
And I'm still waiting here
For you to come back here
But there's a hesitation, I hear
Your voice, hesitant
Who knew you would become my depressant
Suppressing all these emotions
Am I still your weapon
Go and dim the lights
I'll still be asking what happened
Between me and you
The seed that once grew

That once bloomed
Has met its doom
So come on
Tell me the truth
Am I your legend, a home run
An imitation of Babe Ruth
Do you celebrate the smoking gun
Is this all for fun?
Is that why you're on the run?
And I'll still be here
Watching you over there
Once I was royalty
Now you're questioning your loyalty
Each day, a little later
I'll keep waiting, leaping down from ladders
Where do I land? Do we disregard each other
Like we're mouth washing to the vacuum of space, neither
Of us wanting to admit the problem
Your disregard, a venomous weapon
Stuck in this corrupted system
Writing holy scripture into linen
You were once the captain, now you curled
Under the wait of the voyage
And with the weight of my world

You bared the package
If I'm a stain in your teeth
And you have to wash me clean
Why even let me in?
Is this how it's always been?
I'll be waiting for you to orbit back
But I'm losing hope in that
What is fiction and fact
What do we lack?
Is it really me you want?

To
Leah Johnson

Your Will

Sadly, Mickeal

Is that a sign in your eyes
Is that where our love goes to die?
You live to fill me with sorrow
And I live to hope for a better tomorrow
And if you are to leave in the end
Then why do you bother to pretend
Is that a knife in your hand
Where our love finally bends
Say that you love, but I know that you don't
Say that I'm the problem, admit it, you won't
Rearrange it, but change it you don't
Say it's in my head, but I'm not your want
Is that a glimpse in your eye
Is that where you loved die
Is this when I realize
That this is all a guise
Let the impulse to love
And the impulse to hope

Bring us above
And you say you'll change, but fly away like a dove
This garden is rotten
And there's nothing holding
Me together, fractured and broken
Rust on a chalice, once so golden
Love me, well I know that you don't
Empty, I know that you won't
Love me again, I know that you don't
Have the same want and won't
Ever want to show some decency
Or some urgency
As if you pay homage to agencies
My feelings have no importance
To you, again
And I will pretend
And again
I will bend
Then break under all this heartache
If I had a feeling, would I be your headache?
Where we always destined to separate
Was everything destined to complicate
Well, drag me under
Drown me in holy water

Erase me into vapor
Drown me in your holy water
Once my savior
Well I know, that I will sink
To the trenches of our sea
Well I know, as I blink
It's plain to see
You drag me under
One after another
Sinking, either
I let you drag me under
Or I learn how to get this feeling from another
Person
This feeling has been long in its lurking
Is it the end of this show? The curtain close
And you disregard my hurting
Aching bones as they crack
Crumbling In the aftermath
I sink to the bottom of that
Ocean we had laid flat
Drag me under, as I sit under the thunder
Drag me under, as I enter my final slumber
Drag me under, ambulance sirens like thunder
Drag me under, this medicated slumber
And I know that in the end

It was just a game of pretend
And I know, that in the end
I don't have to pretend
Because you don't care
You wouldn't dare
Consider to care
This love, now my waking nightmare
Collapsing under the weight
Of this cryptid
A manifestation of our fate
This story we fabricate
As I sink under
You'll look for another
Person to drag under
Another
Victim to lure into slumber
Another strike of your poetic thunder
Let me fall into my slumber
I can not take another day of this weather
And I know, this is my fault
I know, this is what it was about
And I know, this is my fault
I know, this is what it was about
As the medication dries my throat
You ate everything like a goat

And you'll sail away on your boat
Like our love was something to bloat
And still, there's a part of me
That wants go feel your presence
And still, there's hope in me
That I am something more in your existence
That I am not regret
Nor a burden
That you can forget
That I am not your weapon
And use me once more
And unlock this vault door
If this is a game, and I'm in your way
Let's play, this final masquerade
And somewhere, deep inside this husk
Is some sort of hope for us
And as they load me into the ambulance
I'm nothing but a rotting husk
Will I be your favorite regret?
Or something you'll forget
Tangled with all my regret
And if I awake, I hope to forget
And if I wake up in a hospital bed
I'll still want to be dead
And as I wake up in the hospital bed

I know, that a part of me will be dead
So put on your poker face
Inhabitants the same space
Wait back at my place
Betting on my losing race
And out there
Is maybe the love you're looking for
And right here
I'm still wishing for more
And right here
I collapse under the door
And right here
I lay behind The ambulance doors
In a way, I wanna roll the numbers
In a way, I ignore the numbers
In a way, I wish for another
Chance to win your indifference
To make a difference
I showed you my weakness
I plagued your existence
I blame myself for the resistance
Maybe I should have been more hesitant
I'm stuck with you, you got a captive audience
I'm not a lover, just a resident
In this panopticon of a fortress

Tangled with what I never said
And burdened but what you'll never say
Suffocating with what I never said
Knowing that I will always be in your way
This is just reality
I wasn't meant to be happy
And somewhere in my schemality
My bloods pumping
The poison that was suppose to make me happy
And I'll be left with this crimson reality
And somewhere, in another reality
I'll be the thing to make you happy
To make you satisfied
Not crucified
Not terrified
Well, only terrified
If you actually cared
I guess I lost the dare
To myself, I don't care
So how do I dare
For you to feel the same
As we play the bushes game
Beating around it And it's name
Hiding all our pain and shame
And somewhere out there, maybe

There's hope for us, probably
Some other reality
Where I can make you satisfied and happy
I want to love you so badly
But that's not in the cards of this reality
I want to love you, but sadly
There's nothing left for us in this reality
And I know you'll move on to someone else
And forget my very existence
Reeling someone else into your trap
Exploiting their weakness
How did you grow to be so manipulative
How did I grow to be your directive
I can't see your perspective
But yet, I try to be respective
And we'll keep playing
As the breeze keeps swaying
Our sails, so that's why
I'm taking my life away
Ending this misery
I'll just be apart of trivial history
The spark and conflagration of your misery
The addition of all you bury
And you'll leave with a hurry
As I submerged Into the trenches

My body laying on the stiff benches
Nature made in those trenches
Always met with my repentance
I want to be a salvation
But how can I save you
If I can not save me
And the bottoms so dark, can't see the blue
I can not expect to save me and you
Stuck in your tar trap fortress
Stuck In your path, boundless
My excuses, meaningless
Knowing that none of this matters
So I should stop the literary ladders
Balls in your field, go to batter
And I'll still be waiting, even when you find another
Person, a fly in your target trap
A person, contrast
From the hopeless person I am
That crumbled in the palm of your hand
Come to think of it, was that my weakness?
My own life line and existence
My own need for repentance
My own needs for your existence
Back and forth, we'll play this game

And forget to call each other endearing names
We'll have the same names
Regret and sorrow,
That will be our names
And as the sky cracks down onto the ambulance
I'll be thinking of my repentance
Seizing in your ambivalence
Towards my existence
I made loving you a blood sport
And you'll find a different port
To hunt like a sport
And you'll find a different port
To lay your life in
As you siphon
All of my life in
Your ultimate lesson
And as I think of how to say sorry
For all this caused misery
I know you'll say
It doesn't matter
Because I'll never be anything better
Waiting for you to find another
If you haven't already
Hope they can make you happy
Hope you're ready

To actually be happy
Cause that's something I will never give you
As you sail back into the ocean blue
Show me your weakness
I showed you mine, or is it
My existence
That is your weakness
This game that we play
Ends today

To
Leah Johnson

Reflection

Looking back to this time of my life, I see the warning signs I missed. These feelings that I suppressed, Which would lead to me being depressed, blossomed here. Eventually leading to a death, but not the death of me. Looking back through these letters, I should have known better.

Of course, some of these letters have been edited or adjusted for the publishing world. I don't know why I didn't just let her go at the first warning sign.

Again, I should have known better. *My Hesitation had a reason.*

But now, looking at all the healing I have done, I'm glad to have moved on. The lessons I learned with the experience in this part of my life have truly made me grateful for the man I am today.

And as I move on from this era of my life, and you go on to read the next one, I myself, am finally moving on from this. So in a way thank you.

Not only for purchasing this, but inspiring me.

About The Author

Andi Galupa is an author, artist and musician. But all of her passions share the same need to tell a story, luckily, she has many means to express them through.

Being a trans-woman, she has been through alot in her life, giving her the experience to write the stories she does. Or to explore concepts that people usually won't look deeper into. That is her mission.

To understand the misunderstood.

This Collection

These are a collection of letters I, Michael Hip, wrote to my ex and various other people. I have grown since the beginning of that relationship, but I have a lot more growing to do. Everything has happened for a reason.

This collection I have deemed as "Infatuation.", Picking up where "Hesitation." Left off. On my deathbed, this was a very dark time in my life, but it taught me a ton of lessons that I am grateful for.

So with that in mind, please enjoy.

Till Oceans Tear Us Apart

Yours Apologetically. Mickeal

And I'll wait like the Atlantic
Hidden like Atlantis
You sit by my bedside, this climatic
Storm passing over the pacific
You submerged with me
Am I still enslaved to thee
Merry in the morning
But buried in the mourning
You look down to you feet
Your eyes full of crimson defeat
Waiting for some sort of relief
Maybe I should change my belief
You're just a planet
Orbiting the vacuum I am
I took our love and damned it
The vacuum I am
Consuming all you are
Locked in our prison bars
With all our spare

I'm second guessing who I thought you were
And now, who you are
The nurses talk me through the damage
Tell me the insurance package
Not knowing our treacherous voyage
But hey, I'll keep surviving this voyage
For you, I blame myself
For what I did to you
No one else
But my name to blame what I did to you
Collapse like a temple
Pop like a pimple
All our potential
Destroyed by something so unpredictable
Stuck in your maw, did you forget to eat?
Stuck in your maw, I couldn't taste the feed
Stuck in your maw, I guess you really love me
Stuck in your maw, Is what I see reality?
As you talk me through the labyrinth
That you cared, that you haven't
Left me with this damage
That you too, were famished
This vacuum I am, all consuming
Once blossoming and blooming
Now I'm damning and dooming
This feeling oh so brooding
Flood me with your presence

Wash away the guilt from my hands
Flood me in the present
Take me to foreign lands
Flood me with your presence
Do you understand
What brought us to the present
Did I misunderstand?
I can not bandage up my wounds this time
I cannot hide away, I'm famished this time
I can't bandage the damage this time
A blurred grey line
Don't wait for me
Don't wake me
Don't forsake me
Don't wake me
Up
I don't want to wake up
As charcoal burns in my lungs
Don't wake me up
Numb to my tongue
They pump out the poison
And fill me with fruitful pollen
The walls blue and desolate
This ballad we will replicate
Was this a lie I fabricate
In my state, so delicate
'Till Oceans Tear Us Apart'

Separate chambers of our hearts
Mourning the morning
The doctor walks in
Mourning like the morning
His assessment begins
And I remember when I woke up surrounded
Wolves in white gowns and curses
So high, they had to get me grounded
Wolves, in place of doctors and nurses
Flood me with your presence
Weather me into nothing
Keep me away from the present
I really ruined this thing
That we had going
And above your whimpered shouting
The storm clouds ever brooding
Behind that frown, something was brewing
And calling me to this mourning
The sunlight rising from morning
To the afternoon, still grieving
Fading lightly, afternoon replacing mourning
They ready me for boarding
But I'm still loading
Because you may act worried
But I think something more is brewing
As you break and crumble in your hands
Maybe I misunderstand

Maybe I let you crumble like sand
I apologize, now I understand
They ask me what I want for lunch
But I can't eat
You look at me, hunched
Your what I need
This feelings leading me back to you
And the seed we once grew
Still in that trench so blue
But I'll pretend for you
Sob- once a stoic statue, now at the bedside
Crying on the inside, numb on the outside
Nothing left for us beside
This path, we don't get to decide
And they had me confessing
No, they don't understand why I'm grieving
And their decisions, educated guessing
Really, I'm just grieving
And now through the hospital doors
They ready me for what's in store
Get rid of my laces
But little do they know, I've been to such places
Before
Such familiar doors
If I was present, I'd sink into the floor
I've been here countless times before
Just a different wing of this carrion bird

When I went through those doors
I said I love you, but did I mean those words?
Your face left sobbing behind those pale white doors
Sobbing as I left you, a stitch statue outside
The hospital doors, outside
My eyes sight
Outside of my being
Now fly, fly and levitate
Show me if you still manipulate
Your words and actions, fabricate
Why do we have to slowly complicate
And I wanna say your fake
But honestly, I don't know what to make
Of this facade that you create
Because finally, I capitulate
And let you in
Disregarding all the sins
That happened last time I let you in
These wounds that now, we can not mend
Will you still pretend
That there is some truth to bend?
Or perhaps, I will pretend
And it will all happen again
I dance with a cadence
Akin to sacred
Scripture and as evil as satan
Akin to breaking

Down the molecules of my being
My wounds, they're cleaning
And as the hours pass by
I still know, you will be leaving
Me behind, behind all the ambition In that mind
You were always dreaming, that, you can not leave behind
Leave me behind
If that finally frees your tortured mind
I remember you by the bedside
Sobbing on the outside
But did you feel the same on the inside
On the bedside, your face will always decide
Making me rethink this divide
What is it I should decide
Bodies float to the surface of the water
But I'm still breaking ladders
As the rain pitter patters
Off the oceans waters
And I'all wait, cause our love matters
If not to you, at least to me
And you'll take this matters,
Even if it effects me-
Into your own hands
Sailing out again to more lands
And as I crumble beneath where your statue stands
I hope that maybe, one day

You will fucking understand
What it is like to be this sad
But maybe I shouldn't wish that
Maybe this is just payback
Am I petty?
Cause I know I'm not happy
Are you ready?
To find someone else too obsessively baby
Are you just a fading statue by the bedside
How come that in my own suicide
I'm still concerned more about you, then my own homicide
Ingesting all the poison and pesticide
How come I worry for you and not me
Do I really want to know why that is?
Do you worry, ever, about me?
Is that what it is?
Should I accept it?
Move on and not change it
Just rearrange it
Put down my sword and accept it
I was always some bad at acceptance
I'll crumble in your temple
I'll complicate the simple
I'll worship you as a temple
Until we pop like an abscess pimple
I'll crumble as you fumble

I'll hold you up as I tumble
I'll crumble, I'll crumble
And as long as I can hold you up, I'll be okay to tumble
When the oceans recede, we'll see what lies beneath
The island
And all the seeds we had planted
That we cultivated with our hands
Who else would understand
They've got me surrounded
Yet you stay grounded
They've got you bounded
Yet you'll stay calculated
A stoic statue by my bedside
It's all so complicated
And now you know what I feel inside
I think that's what complicated
And crumbled you like sand
Oh, and when Oceans Tear Us Apart
I just hope to have a fragment of your heart
Just a tiny part
To know, we will never be apart

To
Leah Johnson

Pale Prison

Sincerely, Mickeal Hip

Ladies and gentlemen, doctors and nurses
Mythical scripture and hearses
I've had enough with these lurking
Feelings, like a hawk perching
I feel more than intangible
Not connect to this reality
Feeling unpredictable
My mood swung back from that empty
Feeling in my bones
Cursed, to this home
Even though people are around me, I'm alone
I did something no one can condone
And now the doctors wanna prescribe me this and that
But ignore the long list of facts
Of why I'm back
And surely I do not lack
Reasons for my death
A fresh breath

So unless
I fall upon my literary sword,
You have my word
You fly away on crimson birds
left in this pale prison, visiting the ward
Everyone once in a while
Coldness, that's your style
Seems you care, every once a while
Staring at the walls of pale tiles
Ladies and gentlemen, have you had enough?
Do you know what was really tough?
Debating whether or not I did enough
I've been open handed, was that enough?
Again, disconnected from reality
And I'm feeling more than ready
To disregard your fake apologies
Your like a dagger, symbolically
Small but holding the sharpness
That was my weakness
Using you to fill this emptiness
And as I sit here, questioning my existence
Looking out the window to the free world
Either way I'm enslaved to you
But you keep visiting, saying I'm your world
I feel some clarity, I see through you

And I know how this facade will end
I had been through it again and again
Your staring me down, intimidating to pretend
I've seen it time and time again
And they say I shouldn't be ashamed
But I don't know this feelings name
Staring at the picture with its golden encrusted frames
And the paints saying, "remain
There's a way out of this pain, remain
Hopefully, maybe she will change
Things keep evolving, it's within your range
Now it's time to take this and rearrange
Make your life something more
You been sinking into the floor
Surely, there's something more
For you, in store"
And they're getting ready to discharge
That, I should be looking forward
But I'm not, a little foreword
You say things would be different, after discharge
But I know they won't
Leave? I won't
Hope? I don't
And don't

Tell me all those calculated semantics
And now that I realize your calculations
Spare me all your apologetics
I was dreaming some sort of future, But my predictions
Bring me back into your endless fiction
And as they read my bags
I think of your semantic addiction
And as the rest of the patients call us fags
It's like your dead, talking to our love in a body bag
Do you just see me as some tranny fag?
Just to be thrown away like a torn rag
Pack your care into a bag
Run away, far away
Letting the wind take you away
And I'll remain here, today
Tomorrow and forever in dismay
This pale prison
Taught me the lesson
A corrupt system
And what was that lesson?
I deserve more, but I'll ignore it
For just that addictive love hit
Like a nicotine cigarette

I hate the taste, but can't disregard it
And you'll be waiting for me down the hall
The doctors, standing oh so tall
Make the final, misguided, call
Medicating me without listening to it all
Well Ladies and gentlemen, now you know my secret
I'm open handed, not that you seek it
But truthfully, if dismay is a smell, I breathe it
Looking for a way out, I seek it
There's nothing to gain, nothing to lose
Once I'm home, I'm cracking up some booze
Walk around the garden, now doomed
Remember when it bloomed
Remember when we looked at eachother
Saw something in each other-
Well I do
And for this moment of clarity, your a stoic Statue
You'll remain forever you
And I'll remain forever blue
Now driving home, this angle is half is acute
Something oh so uneven, obtuse
Your probably searching your library for excuse
Spare me the excuse

Cause when I wake up tomorrow, I'll still be miserable
My happiness isn't probable
And to rebuild this bridge is impossible
I'll keep hoping on the impossible
Because I don't learn anything
Always just diving
Into everything
Suffocating
You used to be a god, now a gravestone
I'll bury myself if it means I'm not alone
And as soon as we got home
You left me all alone
No questions, no "How are you?"
No care for me, no impromptu
"I love you"
I'm still trapped in this place with you,
What's there's left to gain?
Is it worth all this suffocating pain
Again, intangible, going off the frame
But here, I will remain
I was on top of the world
All my potential curled
And fell to the ground, hurled
Up with my world

It came crashing down
Sunk into the ground
I gave my everything, I doubled down
And you left me I'm the ground
But yet, you come to the table
Spilling the same old fable
That you'll love me, that you care
But acknowledge me, you wouldn't dare
I guess I'm infatuated with that
Some truth atlas?
Or another lie disregarding the fact
Back to that
You said you sobbed every night
You took the feeling of fright
And tumbled with the fight
This went so far left, not right
Waiting for me to come home
You said, "there's hope in this dome
You're not alone
I love you, down to my bone"
And I want to believe
But I know you'll leave
I just nodded, knowing I will be on my knees
Again, so please
Tell me how you really feel

Show me something so strong, so real
What kind of deal?
How do you actually feel?
But yet, I give you the benefit of the doubt
And let my feelings spill out
You seem surprised what this was all about
And throughout
Our fighting and rumbling
I've been slowly crumbling
While your fumbling
I'm falling and tumbling
Is it foolish of me to believe
That you're not going to emotionally leave?
I want to believe
That you won't leave
I'll keep doing cigarettes
And if you really love me
I'll keep suffering
And if you really love me
As you tell me
I'll believe
Rats in a cage
Trying to stand up brave
In my heart is a grave
Erasing myself and my name

Let me know if this is a facade
A game of charades
If this is a masquerade
Make it the final ballad we'll play
As I sink back into the ocean
I'm falling to your literary potion
I'll believe your notion
Cause your tears sell me the emotion
But is it all calculated?
Statistically fabricated?
Same excuse, copied and pasted
Well, it's my emotions you may have manipulated
But I come to my final consensus
Ignoring my skeptical senses
The census?
I believe you and your calculated sentences
I love you, that's my true feeling
And if it's true what your dealing
And your not just reeling
Me back into feeling
That love that we once grew
From the seed! Who knew
That this would all swing back to you
No matter where I go, it leads to you
I hold my head up high

But I know this could be nigh
The end and the height
Of the stature you created
I was left in the corner
For the coroner
I'm a worshipper
Stuck like an animal in a corner
My action
A final reaction
To believe you, prediction?
Maybe it's all just fiction
But I believe your hook
Can't read you like a book
Cause every time I look
I'm left staring down every crack and nook
And maybe, even though you weren't here for me
You really care for me
Maybe it was all just me
Maybe it is really me
Who's the issue
Crying into soft tissues
Keep waiting for you
Cause I believe in you...
To
Leah Johnson

The . Series 128

Infatuated

Lovingly, Mickeal Hip

I'm absolutely paralyzed
I am infatuated
With you and your will
Wishing there was some magic pill
That would make me Un-ill
That will
Solve all these problems
But this amalgamation of our love
Is now postpartum
The eyes, null of the love
That we had for each other
Recounting the days, as the fade into another
Stoic pattern
And when you leave, I wonder if you'll return
I take my prescription
Never caring for the description
Playing into your fabrication
A victim of your fiction

You will not be mine
But should I be yours this time?
As we sink into the blurring line
Trapped in an endless pantomime
Waiting For you to show, just a smidgen of change
But no, your scared of change
I don't think it's possible for you
Your scared of change
And I am paralyzed to you
You and I are of crashing course
Betting on a losing horse
I'm conditioned to believe your curse
And all of its melodramatic hearse
And I know you will not be mine
And I know, you were never mine
But I am yours
But I'll never be treated as yours
Do you even realize
The pain and suffering in my dull eyes
As our garden dies
Your left, stoic In your lies
Will you please give me something to believe?
Some sort of relief?
Or atleast, take your grip and release?

Is your love for lease?
I would pay anything
To damn your indifference, sacrifice everything
To be treated with some sort of endearing,
everything
That I will never have, everything
You destined to take from me and the world
Destined to be seen positively by the world
And as I work for this cruel, unforgiving world
Stocking shelves and biting scar marks of words
Into my tongue
You'll be the toxins in my lungs
And when we kiss with tongues
I know, that I'll long
For something more
Something, still pounding on your metal door
Something, still waiting for more
Something, something more
Then I think this will ever be
Can you see?
Your indifference is killing me
I thought it would be different, that's killing me
What Could be
And what will never be
Is it all because of me

Will you ever love me?
Or is it all pantomime
Do you shriek at the idea of being mine
Do you always have to be of a lime
A sourness in Indifferent mind
And I know, I'm no one different
I was once hesitant
Now infatuated
As if I am an infant
Looking for your to nurture
To be something more than your stone cold figure
I guess I couldn't see the creature
That I had once asked to nurture
You are not mine
But I am yours
You are not mine
But I will always be yours
Does it hurt you to acknowledge me?
Does it pain you to see?
What has become of me?
They tried to cure me, but couldn't see
The belly of the beast
That swallowed us in its feast
This hollow, horrific beast
Consuming everything in its endless feast

I am paralyzed, thinking of my own will
And I routinely take my pill
But nothing makes it easier to overcome this hill
Cause your Indifference made my life a living Hell
And I'll toss my coins down the wishing well
And you'll keep setting off alarm bells
And maybe, we fell
Into each other as different people
Maybe I'm destined to be trapped in your steeple
Stalking some figment of you and stocking shelves
I'll keep wishing we were as happy as other couples
But my depression will just double
As storm clouds start to envelope
This island, now stone cold in its molecular
Structure, knowing that I can't have savior
When I can't save myself
If you had asked me a week ago
I would have believed something else
I would have played my part in the show
But now there's nowhere else to go
So we'll be left in the winter snow
The final play of our love, we'll it goes to show

We can not love others
When we can not love ourselves
Comparing my self
To every else
And when you reeled me in, you'll put me on the
Trophy shelf
Keep me locked behind the case
Hang the curtain lace
Kick the chair and leave me
In that toxic hell scape
I'll keep looking for escape
In material things, waiting for someone who
Wears a cape
Waiting for a hero, making a fantasy, to escape
This suffering we have made
And all the plots we have played
If we were a show, we'd be rerun
And on the last season, like a smoking gun
We'll keep wondering, what is it we've done?
What is it we ran away from
Was it ourselves or each other
Both looking for another
Person to confide in, another
Keep escaping from each other
Have I become a symbol of your fears?

As you become the river of my tears
Crying a downpours, it's been one year
And yet, we're still here
Do you even want to be mine?
Am I just a set to your pantomime
Do you ever think of yourself as mine
As we keep waiting, time after time
For something different
Do you feel it?
The love that grew into disdain
And how it's wretched taste remains
Do you feel my pain?
Or are you just numb to the fiber in your brain
But here I'll remain
A artwork, trapped in your picture frame
A crashing course of our pain
And endless mirage of some hopeful game
Where there's nothing to gain
Where no one came
To a compromise
Both meeting their demise...
This experience had left me wise
Waiting for you to see me more as a person
And less as a bottom line
Or am I just a person?

In your story, jn your history
You'll keep your heart locked, to my misery
You'll keep the doors shot, predictably
I'm only looking at it statistically
There's a lethal dosage
Mud in our veins, poisoning our voyage
Yet, we act that there's something to cradle
But we'll dig it's grave, and in our voyage
There will be nothing to gein
And in between
Your dismissive indifferent
I'll still be obsessive
Hoping for something different
A hopelessly romantic optimist
Tie the knot, slip some care
Into the envelope, would you dare
Be my vermillion lover
Or treat me as something to snuff, cover
The child of our burning time, where we pray for
A savior
Or at the flick of the lever
Turn blind and eyeless
Are sick, breaking to our weakness
Do you question your weakness
Waiting and bleeding in your indifference

I have waited, and I will continue to wait
Crushed Under the weight
Of your stoic statues plate
Our island, too late
To try to save
Met in a shallow grave
Are we drive by holy force
To ride this vicious horse
And as night befalls the sky,
I'll still look for meaning in those eyes
Never coming to realize
That these are the same recycled lies
And I'll be harvest like rye
You'll catch me, sublime
And in the middle of this winter
We'll enter sleepless slumber
And I'll wait out in vermont
Waiting for all of this to amount
To something we can smile about
But I think there's some doubt
In this fantasy
In you and me
I think we both know the reality
I think you'll always leave me empty
Craving another act to this symphony

Dissonant know it's cacophony
I'm bound to be on my knees
And my thoughts will fall like bees
And I'll crush under these pleas
For you to show some pleasantries
To treat me as a lover
And not just some other
Man to disregard
Sent to you with concerning regards

To
Leah Johnson

Colder Still

Waiting Still, Mickeal Hip

A thousand acres across a delusional desert
Counting my wounds and stabbing the hurt
And every corner this sadness lurks
And every day becomes more and more dark
We're separated by a canyon of indifference
Would you miss me if I ceased existence
And am I the symptom of weakness
Will you always be so relentless
In your apathy
As I keep pleading to the cacophony
Of what once was
And everything that we lived in this fantasy
Will rot compared to what was
I'm struggling to survive
I'm trapped in your eyes
All sense of self has died
I wish I could have realized
That things would not be so dark
But that's a curse of an innocent heart

And I know you will depart
It's a facade, a part
Of a masquerade that never ends
But only, eternally, begins
And as I sit here at the register
Waiting for all of this to register
Ringing me up, in a way, I must forgive her
To try to give her
Some chance, perhaps
Nothing Is what it seems, perhaps
I'm losing feeling in the seams
And I will fade into the serene
Deafening of my screams
Forever waiting
Always debating
As you'll continue manipulating
And I'll still believe you're fabricating
It grows oh so dark now
I took a knee and bow
Under the weight of our false vows
And now I understand, how
One can fall for such a thing
Maybe this was all just a fling
And I'll keep waiting
The island is rotting

But I'll keep waiting
Still waiting
Bow my head under the weight
Crumble beneath the pressures height
With every step, with pain I cry
A divide, not nakedness to thee eye
And everything seems more green on the other side
A difference from what I feel inside
And your colder, still
Like a boulder, still
I'm a stranger, still
Are you still afraid of me, still?
I am not danger
But I'm subject to the creature
That you created in your figure
Singing of my own demise, it lingers
These past weeks, I have grown so wise
I wish I could say I was taken by surprise
With every indifferent reprise
A part of me continually dies
And the night brings you home
But your still leaving me alone
Like your afraid I'll penetrate your bones
With you by my side, I'm still alone

Until I die, until I realize
Locked behind the storm in your eyes
Until I die, from your lies
Sinking beneath the surface of this demise
And still, I'll wait
And still, I collapse under its weight
And still, I'll wait
As you keep leading me with bait
And still, I'll wait
For this story you create
Why do I wait?
When I know it's control you fabricate?
Drowning
Sinking into the ground
Drowning
But your colder still
Suffocating
Our tale keeps complicating
Suffocating
But your colder still
Sub zero
Waiting for you to be the hero
I once knew, still sub zero
And I'll keep waiting
For you to come back to me

And I'll keep debating
If you actually love me
Because lately
And honestly?
It's like you don't see me
That you can't stand that I still be
We'll keep tangling with this divide
And the coldness that lies
Between our moral lines
And in our hesitation, my hope dies
And still I'll create
Some sort of hope, hung by a rope
And still, I'll create
Some fiction of hope, strangled with rope
And every day gets so much harder
And you keep giving me your shoulder
And you keep standing like a boulder
I feel my head becoming so much colder
If I died, would you miss me?
Or be happy?
That I cease to be?
Will you ever acknowledge me?
I'll keep praying to you
Because you're all I have left, that's true
And I'll keep begging you

Till you finally show me a feeling so true
But you'll be colder still
But you'll be a boulder still
But you'll be stoic still
And I sink lower, still
We'll go back and forth
Until we mend our wounds henceforth
Until we bend back and forth
Flowing henceforth
Capitulating to your indifference
Surrendering, cause you'll never be different
At one time I was hesitant
Now I see I'm infatuated
And you'll stay cold
And you'll let this grow so old
A tale already told
And all your excuses have grown some old
Every movement in a font so bold
Alchemizing your being of coal
Into some sort of fools gold
I'll wait for you to not be cold
And my back will succumb to the chill
To The Trenches and treacherous hills
I'll collapse under all these pills
To try to remain somewhat Sane, still

They prescribe me as if their writing a will
And I'll wait at the pharmacy For refill
Knowing that my needs will never be fulfilled
And all my being will be discarded, but still
I'll come home
And bury myself in your bones
Even though, in the end, I was meant to be alone
Standing as a stoic statue, akin to a gnome
And when I awake
If I awake
Another day, to contemplate
If I want to awake
For the sake of me
Let me actually see
If I can be
Anything you want of me
If you even want anything of me
If you even love me
If you actually miss me
If you actually cared for me
Your cold still
This fear your indifference instills
Until I fall upon the sword of will
Can't fix that with endless pills
Encumbered by my existence

Debating a final resistance
In your existential violence
Verbally, I do not strike in defiance
And I'll wait for you at the gate
Left in dismay, in hearts wake
I'll keep looking to the atmospheric cape
Of the sky, the storm above the draped
Metal door
Collapsing to this concrete floor
Locked in your heart, forever more
I'd do anything for something more
That this statue, this silhouette
That lurks around the corners, this silhouette
That I will never forget
It would be a safe bet
That I will come back
Ignoring all the omnipresent facts
And into your shell, you'll retract
And all your disregard will stack
Till I am buried underneath this regret
Did you really forget?
That it was my birthday
Or was it just in your way
To treat me different today
Am I in your way?

Not that you'll let me know
But it's in the actions you show
But it's in the things I know
About everything here, no
I know you'll turn your back
I know you'll prove it as fact
I know I will forever awake
Alone, and after the fact
I will crumble under your presence
And I'll forever be looking to the past,
Disregarding the present
Cold, cold still, freezing, omnipresent
I don't know why I believed anything different
And until I die
I'll be looking for something more in those eyes
And if I died
And the lights fades from my eyes
You'll leave me behind
and erase me from your mind
And I'll keep looking at this divide
Not that you care what's on my mind
Across this divide
You turn your back and leave me behind
I must've not seen it
I had to have seen it

Because I disregarded it
Your indifference
And with every step, I cry
The slits in my wrists, I try
To cover up and shamefully hide
You'll part like the tide
And sail the ocean, like the sky
Levitating above where we once lied
The night is finally nigh
You levitated do high
I'm swimming deep inside your disregard
And I know you will part
And I know, I'll never be in your heart
And what was once sweet, is now tart
You'll always be in disregard
You'll never reside
I've grown so wise
To understand how you feel inside
And until I die, you'll always be trapped inside
And until I die, you'll never show it on the outside
And until I die, you'll never let me inside
And until I die, I'll always be trapped outside
The husk of a garden we created
The indifference, the hating

The death of our fabrication
Met with Your endless fiction
You'll be colder still
Colder still
And I'll still be solving my problems with pills
Waiting up on the hill

To
Leah Johnson

Distracted

Pleading, Mickeal Hip

I'm caught, hook lined and sintered
And from the rain, I hunkered
Down into the pockets of dirt
Line with my disregarded hurt
And if it's too late
If you would care to placate
Give me some sort of distraction
From your endless fiction
Say it with some sort of conviction
Because I want to believe in vindication
But I know this is just a show
Passing like a winters snow
And I know, that you want to go
And leave me in the blistering cold
The oceans frozen over
But you'll still insist, and give me the shoulder
In these past months, I've grown older
And slightly, colder
I'll keep driving myself to distractions

And wishing for some sort of caring action
But it's too late, I'm caught in your infliction
It's too late, I'm beyond your consideration
Not that you had any to begin with
And your figures grow stiff
Once upon a time, I tried to lift
You up, but I fell for it
Your apathetic lack of emotion
Your lack of consideration
Entangled in your fiction
Lost in the friction
We collapse as this crescendo to a head
Leaving us worse than dead
I believed, that I was lead
Into your garden
And you bloomed and pollinated
Before killing and isolating
Me inside all of your desolation
In all of your fiction
I still want to believe in vindication
But every thing never said, makes a reaction
Despite the lack of action
Stuck in a constant cycle of retribution
The evolving devolution
Stuck in your crimson institution

And they tried to cure me
It's too late for me
I've fallen further Into the consuming sea
And every advancement further, hurts me
It's too late for me and you
It's too late, that much is true
I'll fall further
With each passing day, forward
Into tragedy
Sewing together some hopeful fantasy
I was more then you asked for
I was more than you could ever afford
And with every disregard
I watch the love in your eyes part
As if Moses was walking across the crimson
Ocean
And we're just going through the motion
Nevertheless, stoic In our emotion
And I have taken hint with your notion
It's too late for us
No excuses
It's too late for us
I've spent countless days
Hoping for us
Swallowed by this darkness

It's too late for us
Not that you ever saw us
Not that you will ever see us
As we tilt back and forth on this seesaw
And dive into the ocean with the seagulls caw
I am broken, into fractured fragments
And I am due for a harsh punishment
Never seen past your wall of accomplishment
Always disregarding my caring sentiment
And I'll keep feeding my distraction
And I'll be the co-author of your fiction
"No, she's not like any other
She gave me the power
And truthfully I love her
She doesn't see me as the same as others"
I'll keep lying to myself
Like I'm someone else
And this walls will watch me belt
My sorrows and all that I felt
Numbed by alcohol
My destruction is probable
Coming back is impossible
It's too late for me, it's impossible
To make a come back
When I can't separate fiction from fact

And with all the feelings you lack
I'll keep looking over the fact
As we fall, diving further
This storm, I can no longer endure
And I am just a silhouette of a creature
And as we fall further
You'll dismiss me once more
Locking me from your hearts door
And I'll submerge once more
Saying there's something more
Something in that husk of a women
That has now become a coping system
Who is the solution to my problem
The stoic statue of a women
And I'll fall upon my sword
Pleading the same words
As you fly with the birds
Here are my warmest regards
Truthfully, it's too late for me
Oh can't you see
Your indifference hurts me
And now, it's too late for me
And I'm suffocating
Everything, defenestrating
Me to your manipulating

And I'll hold my breath, even though I'm
Suffocating
Is it too late for me?
Will you ever see
The person you once filled with glee
Will you ever see
That you killed that glee
Will you ever see
Your killing me
Will you even hear my sleep
Or pretend to be deaf
To these crippling beliefs
Searching for some sort of sign of relief
Take your grip and release
I want to be free
I want to be me
I want to want to be
How can you not see?
Between romantic fantasies
And bottles of hennessy
We live two different realities
With separate themalities
Was I something you asked for?
Or will you always shut the door
Are you waiting for something more

Is it something I can actually afford?
Breaking me down
Bury me in the ground
Crumbling down
Have you found
All that you have looked for
Still, I'll scream at that door
Till it opens, begging
Pleading on the floor
It's too late for me, descending
Your moving on, ascending
It's too late for me, foreboding
Your moving on, transcending
Your moving on from me
And I'll never be as free
As you will feel
When you discount me as real
Did I amount to how you feel
Was this all fake? Never real?
I am broken, fractured
I am broken, quartered
Try to forget, distracting
Trying not to regret, retracting
Another bottle down
As I bury our love in the ground

Oh, and truly she wasn't like any other
Truly, she was like my mother
Truly, she'll leave like my father
And I will always be a nuisance, a bother
She will forget everything
Searching for something
That I can't be, everything
That's what I'd give, anything
To change your attitude
To get some sort of gratitude
It's too late for gratitude
That's the mood of your attitude
Forget me already
I know your ready
To sail the seas with your indifference
Forsaking my very existence
Forget me, move on
The damage is finally done
Forget me, move on
You hold the gun
Annihilate me, move on
You were always on the run
Obliterate me, move on
Because whether your here or not
You'll always be gone

But don't worry about me
I know you're indifferent to me
I understand what your body language means
I'm a stain of which you will clean
Something to never be remembered
To think I could love you forever
But now our love is dismembered
And I should of acknowledge that, never
Did I acknowledge that
The empathy you lack
As I smoke my final pack
Trying to heal these scars in my back
You pulled out the knife
You took my life
But I survive
Now with this crumbling strife
I am driven to distractions
Turning my senses
Into fractured fractions
The final consensus
It's too late for us
No more excuses
It's too late for us
No more uses
And I know you'll forget us

It's too late for us
Go on, forget us
It's too late for us
Go on, undo us
Entangled like the crucifix and Jesus
Go on, forget us
Walk on water, female Jesus
Go on and show your prophecy
Go on and heart the red sea
Go on and your about me
Go on and be free
And I'll remain broken
And I'll see myself as the problem
Forever stuck in your system
Remaining broken

Surrendering To
Leah Johnson

Bleed Me Dry

Regretfully, Mickeal Hip

I'll take shelter from the shade
And watch the sun in the sky fade
You were once wearing a cape
Now it hangs as a curtain drape
We can't repair the damage done
But confessions, You'll run
Because you have no honesty, none
And as I stare down the bottle of rum
I know that there's nothing left
To all we forget
Tangling with this emptiness
Burdened by my existence
If I wake up, put me back to sleep
If slumber is what I need
Make sure I never feed
Starving, those eyes are a book to read
Threading the bead
A necklace for my empress
Conquering, as I bleed
I'll forever be a weakness

You must terminate
Because all I do Is complicate
This bottle of hennessy
Brings this fantasy to reality
And now I see, death is not an enemy
But a release from this nightmarish reality
And as I pray to never wake up again
Excited for this perpetual end
Praying and begging again
But the man up there has given me my end
Infinitely, I will bleed
Never one to read
Holy scripture
Outcasted As a estranged creature
Unholy fixture
It's not a bug, your indifference is a feature
And as I dig my grave with my hands
Vultures circle above our land
Disease is the end of gardens
But that's oversimplifying the problem
A stinging feeling in my teeth
Like bleaching to a reef
Like mouthwash, like anya, to me dismissed
All my pleas, echoing in the abyss
We climbed ladders, I bow my head and submit

We'll drown in the foamy abyss
What a world for our children
Where we crush under narcissistic systems
Blaming ourselves for the problems
I guess I'm just a mess
Tangled with my emptiness
You have become my silver lined weakness
I didn't mean to complicate your existence
And even now, I'm hesitant
Was I ever your fantasy
Or just a well meaning enemy?
What is reality?
Are you ready?
To let go of me, forget me
And beneath the starry sky
I can finally see
What I saw in your eyes
The day we met
Beneath all these lies
Did you forget
The warmness I once saw in your eyes
Or was that all a disguise
Now I have grown ever wise
What is there left but demise?
From ashes we rise

Only to love a person we despise
Is there nothing left but eulogy
A shallow grave, a sense of formality
In an ending of this reality
The light has faded on this fantasy
Living in this empty place
Numb to my face
When I close my eyes, and forget the race
You'll finally meet the pace
That I am holding you back from
As we dance this endless prom
Separate accounts of a form,
Now, carpe diem
Leave me with all my decisions
When they do the autopsy incisions
Ask them if they could feel my emotions
The lack of, and in these literary notions
I'm flailing And falling
Back into the trenches of the sea
And as the ocean balloons
I can now see, this is the end of me
And to the marching of my heart beat
I see the end of me
The precipice of defeat
The end of eternity

And all we have to lead
Is a hopeful project
That we dream of, asleep
Lying to ourselves that love is all we need
Yet, still asleep
We don't know how to feed
We collapse, falling upon our feet
Preaching of our own defeat
Sayings we endlessly bleat
You watched me cry, now watch me bleed
You'll rise above the waves
You'll pledge that your brave
But who else is to blame?
Do you even remember my name?
Hollow and empty
Begging and tempting
I crash upon the ocean floor
And the last thing I see, a locked door
But you had the keys
You never planned to give them to me
The keys
As I overdose on what could be
I'll keep watching you leave
Breaking me
Your silence leaving me free

To think of what could be
A perpetual end, a nuclear winter
The trees providing a temporary shelter
Before cut down, and the coldness of this war
Realizing that maybe, you're ambitions whore
Never satiated, always wanting more
And what's truly in store?
Can I never be something more
Hide behind your cellar door
I'm done knocking
Your done talking
And as I cease walking
You'll still be lying
The ambulance sirens in the distance
A cure to your indifference
The ceasing of my burdening existence
I'm giving up all resistance
So go on and levitate
Because we both know I complicate
And we both know, we'll fabricate
And look for something manipulate
Neither of us are so different after all
We'll both fall
Your stoic sobbing echoing off the halls
Suffocating beneath all your walls

There's nothing left
Everything, you must forget
Staring into the void
How can beauty be devoid
Of the color
Making pale whites a feature
As we finally bleed to back
And the aftermath
If I come back
Give me a pack of cigarettes
So I can clear my lungs of the poison
And if you actually listen
Tell me if I was the problem
Breaking like the waves
A feeling of resolve
Done with all the rage
And If I was the person you were destined to hate
Leave me beneath the crashing tide
And Island wise
Bury me with what we planted
The answer I demanded
Never came
Cause you never gave
But just take
Take take take

Till there's nothing left of me
There's nothing more to see
Crushing under the sea
Poseidon's trident burying me
We fell upon our promises
Leaving our premises
This demise implicit
Motions, we are so complicit
I've made what I meant explicit
Now don't forget it
And now sinking into midnight
The light, it tries to fight
We went so far left, it felt right
A orchestration of a playwright
Like the ending of Macbeth
This all comes to a head
On a pike, is our love
The mass extinction of doves
Nevermore, the raven caws
Nevermore, above everything I saw
I see now that we're failing the test
And even though we may have given it our best
There is no remedy
You'll still be making enemies
Fabricating realities

Manipulating fantasies
Death is not our enemy
But merely a savior
And what will I be?
But a passing memory to her?
And what did she see?
But a broken cog
And what did I see?
A feminine God
Who will bleed me dry
And no matter what I try
My brain is just fried
But at least I tried
To unlock the door
That I had been pound on, nevermore
A taste of something more
For you, somethings in store
For me? Nevermore
And now, henceforth
I'll cease to move forward
Cause no matter what, I'll move backwards
Wearing your care as a dress
Taking it off when you need a rest
There's nothing left
So don't waste your calculated breath

Because you wished for my death
And prayed for my downfall
I saw it, written among the walls
The writings in the halls
The house has fallen
And now usher
A new forever
Will I even be remembered?
Was I just a burden
A snake caught in your system
Inflicted with your venom
And was I the problem?
Or just a ward of the mental health system
What did I see in you as a woman
Because this soured into a demon
A rotting watermelon
Go trap someone else in your system...
And all we'll ever be
Is a collapsing tide in the sea
Bouncing off our disbelief
One of us was destined to leave
And all we'll ever be
Is just a crimson fantasy
This is the end of my reality
Hope you appreciate the formality

Go on and levitate
Without me

To
Leah Johnson

Wilting Rose

Surviving, Mickeal Hip

I woke up in the hospital bed
Hoping they would pronounce me dead
Fading like the act you shed
Sitting a next of my death bed
Sobbing, as if a tsunami
Crashed against the island
Do you actually mourn me, solemnly?
Do you actually understand?
As I fade into the nothing I am
This tragedy goes hand in hand
With The death of our island
Worms crawl out of the open can
I know how this goes
I can predict the end of this show
And who would ever know?
We'll collapse under the question, proposed
You're an illusion
And in my delusion
You'll fade, a framed illustration

That's fact, not fiction
The doctors tell me the damage
I'm lucky to have survived such a voyage
But I'm sad, and I know this will be used as leverage
You'll farm this for it's harvest, pepperidge
And now, high as a kite
This feeling, my body fights
Leading me with the fading lights
They read me my patient rights
Only a few months past
And I'm back here at last
Everything's happening so fast
And I'll lose my hope on this path
This weight on me, collapse
Addictions, I'll relapse
Everything on the insides out, prolapse
And we'll forever be victims of the moons eclipse
Stuck in this cycle forever
Saying, knowing that this will never
Last for now, or forever
Knowing that we will never
Be the same
All victims to this game
You say my name

With a calculated
Manipulating sentiment
Did we not see the consequence
Is this eternity God's punishment?
And as they carry me through those pale white doors
And the sanitized, white washed floors
Like I'm a product in a convenience store
They'll ask "what brings you once more?"
And I'll lie and say "the meds didn't work"
But there's a deception in those words
And I'll look outside to the migrating birds
Dancing to dissonant alerts
My ears becoming deaf from the dissonance
Lost in the frequencies resonance
Same room, same residence
I'm poisoned, your my weakness
Inside your facade you hide
But I know the creature under the tide
I know that your demeanor will slide
A mood swing like a legato glide
I followed you to my death
I let you infiltrate my head
And now, I'd rather be dead
Then be alive to have you in my head

You might be indifferent, but that's not what is killing me
It's the fact that the illusion of you enslaved me
Locked the door and threw the key, set me free
This cold concrete prison is killing me
And they keep asking what happened?
Why I had faltered and fallen
Upon my defeated, my heart swollen
Choking on poison and pollen
To you, I am nothing
I'm staring through the telescope
Looking for some sort of regeneration
But I guess it's a generation's of danger
I fall upon my vices, Dicker addison
And my worlds collapsing
All this is conceptually adding
And I'll be subtracting
My self from this equation
I've stared at the chalkboard
Until the nonsense becomes words
I'm confused, as you levitate with the birds
And migrate to other worlds
I look at the window
Knowing nothing will change tomorrow
And I'll wallop in my sorrow

Nothing changes, yesterday, today or tomorrow
You infiltrated my bone
I wanna tell them, but that won't bring me home
You visit me, but I still feel alone
I lifted you above all else, 'neath the cracking of my bones
And now as I sit in my room
Recounting my repeated doom
I watch this horror bloom
You always return at the same time, noon
And I dreadful when that time arrives
Because like the sea, you'll part
I know this cycle, I'm your disregards
And everything you say, guarding
Our love, tainted by stoic defeat
And I know when you leave
You'll feel some kind of relief
That's my belief
Burdening your soul
Taking and taking with each pull
Pushing me out into something so null
Lost to the ocean in your skull
Pulling me back into your arms
Ignoring all the warning alarms
And I'll be a cat in your barn

Trapped forever in your stone heart
And I know, when you part
That I bring you to a place so dark
If this was a taste, I'd be tart
Like I'm a shopping cart
A price you will never pay
An obstacle in your way
And as the crimson trees sway
You'll plunge me into shade
And as I begin to fade
I wonder why you came today
I keep putting that on replay
You a heaven and hell?
The two faced well?
The ringing of deaths bell
As we climb up the knoll
And is this dance the only thing we know?
And is this all we will know?
Will I never escape, move onto someone else
If. above nothing else
Trapped in the blizzard snow
With nowhere left to go
So what's to show?
But the feeling of the beast below
We fall for this trickery

Hexxed in your wizardry
And I'll be forgotten history
Responsible for this temporary misery
Their extending my stay
So they can take my feelings and placate
Unsure of what date
Discharge will take place
And I'll keep grappling with this dismay
If it means I won't be in your way
So I'll put my sword and law
Beneath the roses thorns
As you will scorn
Our love torn and worn
Something in this death was born
Something new, something we knew
A rebellion, a feeling oh so new
And now I know I'm not the person you thought you knew
I'm done being oh so low
Sick of being below
I've came for what you owe
Your empathy and ending of this show
No love? No loss, no details to gloss
No love? Stuck in your spirit box
No love, no loss, am I getting my point across

I have to detach and toss
You with my warmest disregard
Once sad, not angry in part
This fantasy we larp
Falling upon you crimsoned sword
I'm not the first, won't be the last
Now I see why we moved so fast
You weren't expecting this to last
Like an orgasm, the pleasures passed
And now we're left empty
Well, at least I'm empty
Your love was statutory
But that's not the end of the story
A feeling has overcome me
Rising above this misery
The powers within me
Enduring you history
Forsake me, forget me
I'm history
And now I see
You really ate like the sea
You rise and fall like the tide
And it was only coincidence
That we collide
Now I see, the warning, the reason I was hesitant

And the person I relied
The person becoming a symbol of indifference
The person by my bedside
Was not the person I thought
The person that I fought
The person I appreciate
The person I thought
Felt the same
But It was all a game
Just another name
On the list and frame
Picture perfect is how you hold yourself
Because nobody else
Will ever be like yourself
This spite, above all else
Has come to me like a wave
I'm feeling brave
Your indifference is depraved
This path we paved
I was waiting for something else
But that never came
I died waiting for something else
But it never came
And now, I'm eternally awake
I overcame

The feeling when I was awake
It came
But didn't last
Cause now your in the past
Just a street to pass
On my road to my definition of success
Recount your excuses
The sentiment, countless
Your stoic being, infectious
When you come to visit, and talk of us
I see right through you, window
You don't care about tomorrow
You don't feel sorrow
Your just- spiteful
It's regretful
That in your eyes, I'm forgettable
Is reform impossible?
Or somewhat probable
And is it worth the time
To try to make you mine
Thats a grey, blurring line
A fight we must entwine

To

Leah Johnson

Olive Branch

Peacefully, Mickeal Hip

This fantasy, I couldn't shake
A slumber from which I will never awake
It started mundane enough
The weather and thought
That if I sat with my loathsome ignorance
The feeling would not be such a depressant
Growing weary of the taste and resistant
And I had this recurring dream where we
weathered the storms bombardment
Swept under the rug, to never me acknowledged
My suffering reaching its threshold,
consequential
Your indifference, illuminating my unease
As if all autonomy has been abandoned
And now I see, you are the thirst, never quenched
You are the hex, the problem and the wrench
You are the sky and the oceans grew
You are the concrete beneath the bench

And as I extend this olive branches
I'll still dream of our garden's ranch
This recurring fantasy
Where you don't treat me as an enemy
And we love each other honestly
Instead of running cowardly
And when this dream succumbs me
Covered in a smoke downfall
I see this hope, become me
The wind roaring at the windows
Like clockwork, you come out of the shade
The ocean in your eyes, now a crimson fade
You are the fire that will never relent
You are the curse to never repent
And there's still a fragment
Something in there, but consequence
Ways in it's wise balance
The shifting states of killing
Paranoid, now that's present tense
And as the fluorescents
The lights, illuminating my unease
Falling upon my sore knees
But something different
A clarity I can see
And as the wind taps on the window panes

And the gold melts from the picture frame
I see now, we are loathsome fools
Not playing by our set rules
And as they medicate me into a drool
I'll still ballon like a fool
But will you change?
Is that something you can arrange?
Or is that just so- deranged?
Is it my sorrow you will cauterize
And now I see, through the gaps in the trees
The ghastly pale seas
And the flickering of loves flame
This feeling, once shame
Now understanding your game
And the weight of your name
Did you love me like a dream?
And when you awake
Did you forget the feeling, serene?
And as I awake
I hand this note to you
To show me a feeling so true
Because I caught fire for you
And now I burn for you
As we delve into the depths of this tragedy
Show me, fact, show me reality

Stop playing me like a fiddle In your fantasy
Show me some sort of truthful formality
And as your eyes become less of a looking glass
But more of a poignant mirror
I'll keep begging to the past
To bring it nearer
But the image, muddy in its grain
Never gets clearer
Change the frames
But it will never be clearer
Just a product for your shelf
Just a illusion of self
An ego death, felt
Deep within your bones, left
For the world to ponder
From the path, we will wander
We take the prices and sauder
Some sort of eternal slumber
And as we move closer to December
Do you remember?
What this once was
What this once, could have been
This was
Unforeseen
Trepidation seals our fate

With this taste we both hate
An exit, we can create
Something to shield us from the pressure of the storm
And as I become my weakest form
I see now, on this watery sphere
That this became the thing we fear
If we last a year
Will you really be here?
That's what I ask for
For something more
Something to be excited for
Something more than a lock door
Locked forevermore, nevertheless
I will obsess
Waiting for you to confess
Will you repent?
As I do the same
Choking upon your name
But we can change that
Even if it's after the fact
Maybe cause the statue to crack
Before the stoicness creates a lack
Of emotion, sympathy or empathy
This final epiphany

Waiting for you to end the symphony
And as we move closer to tragedy
My discharge looming heavy
As for me? I am not ready
Using materials to fill this space that's empty
And we'll keep tempting
Or at least I will
As you had instilled
And as the night becomes still
We have both fallen ill
In separate ways
Living separate days
Caught In separate sways
Looking upon the stars, believing In the mystical of fae
I keep mentioning this recurring dream
But let me finally paint the scene
It's a collateral matter, destroying all time and space
One that brings a satisfactory smile to my face
Void of suffering and a pace
That outlasted this coalition, racing
With the sun, revolving around something more
Then a broken promise and a locked, Steel door
Something that breaks the ceiling and the floor

Something that amounts to much more
Then the statue your insistent on being
Something of higher power, higher being
A nirvana In a single action, something of meaning
And a cease to all this cleaning
A need to not erase but create
Without needing to fabricating
Forgetting to manipulate
Something sustainable to create
Maybe I'm a loathsome fool
Who doesn't believe in the rules
Maybe I'm a loving fool
Who keeps ignoring all the rules
That teach us this game
But I hope to be more than a name
Something more than your dismay
Stumbling in the storms way
It will pass, and as the night sways
We'll want to be the sun in eachothers days
Abandoning autonomy
Becoming one in figurative anatomy
Such a foolish fantasy
I believe, I can bring into reality
Because this is not the precipice of our eternity

But the passing of temporary tragedy
It's plain to see
And I hope that you can join me
This olive branch, proliferate
By the words, separated
From my feelings of disdain
A feeling that can not be sustained
Inside my head is where I sat
Till I became fat
Of the fear and lack
Of nutritional snacks
A taste I was quick to spit
Into this bonfire we lit
A conflagration that will not let us forget
A character of madness, unless
We get through this passing storm
We get through this roaring storm
We try to survive the storm
But we are consumed in its chaotic form
And here, in my fantasy, you call my name
Without the weight of your indifferent shame
A warm, sun like comfort in the calling of my name
The capitulation of this game
Such a beauty should be framed

Such a fantasy must be named
And we can not remain
In this constant disdain
We sink into the depths
As we leapt
From buildings, never to forget
The very depths
Of my concern, if you have any to show
My concern, knowing that no
One can ever know
The sweet person you refuse to show
That's the person I fell in love with
The one who became stoic and stiff
The one that I can not forget
The one who the fire lit
In a world of darkness, fading
This madness of our regret, draping
The colors meld Into one, shading
This once dark world, foreboding
Flickering my unease
The Ignoring of my pleading
I'm not wasting anymore time asking
No longer am I begging
And I refuse to keep bleeding
And we'll fall upon our swords

Forever cursing the shame of our words
The colliding collapsing weight of worlds
As our fates where curled
Entangled into one, will love win?
If we refuse to let it in
Like it's something to be sold in a discount bin
Is it something you're scared to let in?
Do you actually wish to see me forevermore
In reality, do you hide behind your hearts door
Do you actually wish we could be something more
Or do your sadistically want to see me collapse to the floor
Two attempts to erase myself
Two attempts too many, hating myself
But now I see, above all else
That it is not my fault, it is the result
Of your indifference
Your need for constant status
Once we lose this division, and love our names
Once we give up our charades
Then we will reach the precipice of eternity
Forever, cursing this formality
And either we'll catch on fire
Or prevent the burn...
To

Vultures

Pleading, Mickeal Hip

Cast the shadow I let in
Believing all your excusing reasons
As you facade changes like the seasons
And before this all begins
Where do I turn
Because these vultures burn
Standing on the ferns
Dead and rotting, forever burn
Keeping myself numb
Pretending that I am dumb
Out of the hospital, but to these wound, I still succumb
You bled me till I was dry, what has this become?
Is this me? Is this figure a creation
All of this questioning, and illusion
Is it time to run, what's the right decision?
Will I always suffocate in your confusion?
Do I lay down and die
Closing my eyes

Because all around me, are pretty white lies
And for so long- I have realized
That I am a trophy in your case
Nothing more but a face
And once your done with me, you'll replace
Your trophy, vultures circling
This cycle forever churns
These vultures, circling
How the tables forever turn...
Forget everything, forget my name
It's all apart of this game
Discharged, papers signed with the doctors name
Nothing resolves, just a hair in your mane
The lion's roar, your life, I spectate
Trying to replicate
The lion's roar, you act as if we are separate
Will you ever see me as an equal part?
Or do you sink with your stone heart?
Am I destined to play this part
A spectator in your life, never to be let into your heart
And it's not that I hate you, it's that I hate myself
For letting you become the only figure in my life
And if there is nothing else
Blow me away, take the knife

Take aim, you'll continue to levitate
Take aim, I'll continue to capitulate
Take aim, every situation, a station to manipulate
And I'll fall upon my sword, fabricate
Some sort of story to believe
Some sort of fake release
Never to acknowledge me
Deciphering what your body language means
But as the shadows cast over the horizon
I'm still struggling
Looking at the fading sun on the horizon
And your still disregarding
And I don't know, whether you want me
Or whether, you need me
Need me to just leave
So you can be
And I pretend to close my eyes
And I pretend to sleep
But each and every day, a part of me died
I can't stop myself from being awake, what do I need?
Will I forever be asleep?
Will I always be destined to leap
Back into your arms, where collaterally, we meet

And am I destined to unrealistically believe
That you will change for me
That you will care for me
Because, for so long, I've been waiting for a light
Waiting for a time that is just so right
And somewhere inside me, there is a fight
Quenching the thirsts plight
You're cold, you're bitter
You're bold, you're better
You're spiteful, forgetful
Yet I'm hopeful, and grateful
I'm destined to be jaded into belief
As your indifference is relief
What's left to burn? You've taken everything from me
Is there anything left but to sleep?
Should I close my eyes?
Because without each passing day, I die
Waiting for you to orbit back to me
Why do I still believe?
And you'll steal my breath, running into the distance
As I surrender all resistance
Bathing in your indifference
Searching for something in your hesitant

Confusion, overwhelms me
Division, quells me
Forsake me
Forget me
Take aim, you vultures
Take aim, leave me out of your culture
Take aim, you pessimistic destroyer
Take aim, take aim, there's nothing left but to slumber
And truthfully, the colors have faded
I've done more the participated
I've tried not to spectate
But I feel so jaded
So take aim, annihilate me
So take aim, obliterate me
And when the ocean collapses Into the earth
You'll still be the definition of all of my worth
So take aim, vultures
Take aim, I'm a mere creature
Subject to your manipulation
Lost in your two faced conviction
And I'll keep hoping that the wind will blow
And I'm still hoping for an end to this show
And we both know
I can not hold my breath forever, no

And I'll collapse to the circling vultures
The garden, met with desolation
I live to appease those vultures
I live to believe your manipulations
Like I'm weighing down your levitation
I just need some gratification
Cause I'm lost in this confusion
And vultures feed of this conviction
That you don't care
That you can't bare
To even look at me, to acknowledge I'm there
As if you did, is that what you fear?
Or Is there a iceberg underneath
These walls of our home reek
Of the coldness we breed
Is there something underneath
Cause all I can see, sitting on my bed
Waiting for you to care if I was dead
And your indifference is getting into my head
What is there left?
For so long, I have waited For you to change
And right when I go to leave your range
You say you'll make some sort of change
But now I just see, your excuses rearrange
Where do we go from here? Bad blood

Wishing things could be different, lost In its flood
Let go, but I don't know, hoping is in my blood
Where do we go from here? Where do we go? Lost
in your flood
But I'll waiting, building arcs out of dying trees
Lost in the blistering breeze
Upon your isolation I freeze
And right when I go to leave
You pull me back in, it might be to late
You set a specific time and date, but your late
No longer can I pretend yo placate
This suffocating feeling you make
These excuses we create
This care you fabricate
I'll wait for the oceans to collide
Lost in its forever rising tide
Would you care if I died?
Would you know if I lied?
Or are you afraid yo care at all
Your vultures tear apart my body
I've lost all autonomy
Take aim, destroy me
Take aim, am I the enemy?
Vulturous, destroy me
Vulturous, can you ever acknowledge me

And will I forever wait for change?
Will everything always rearrange
Will you always bring such dismay
Sinking into the oceans sway
Pulled beneath the cacophonous wave
And this storm, I try to brave
A watery, unmarked grave
Can you show some happiness saying my name?
Or is it such a burden to weigh
Is it a burden in your way?
Is It fiction like the fae?
Our swords, we lay
But the roses prick my thumb
As I grow oh so numb
I can not play dumb
These words, we will succumb
This can't be all that's left for us?
Falling for that act, countless
Sick of your endless excuses
And I will run with the wind, Infectious
So count my time, following your misdirection
Lost within your two faced conviction
Digging deep For some meaning in your objection
Some sort of meaning, rotating convection
And if I was to lay down and die

I would accept that it is my time
Searching for meaning in those dull eyes
A facade we will forever mime
Is there something more underneath?
Is there some sort of feeling towards me?
Is there nothing left to be
Am I just damned to believe?
And all I see is dull, grey shadows
Decorating the walls and suffocating the shallows
Where I keep hoping, for better tomorrow's
But I'll be forever stuck in your minds gallows
But yet, just attempt to hold my breath
Hoping for the sweet release of death
A breeze to catch my breath
And in your indifference, I'll freeze to death
Your indifference bleeds onto the pages
Is there something that changes?
When I tell you how I feel
Do you have any idea how real
These feelings are
And as you burn the passion, I can't bare
To watch our love die...
Caught in your endless conviction
As if I'm drawn to intoxication
Cash my skin, sell my fur

As we push our indifference further
Into the depths of this creature
The beast beneath films feature
And when I lay down a next of you
I just feel so blue
Crimson, that's what I see in you
Knowing that your love isn't true
I'll let you clamp down your jaw
Until you bleed me dry
Forever trapped in your maw
And everytime I try
Your indifference gets to me
Your ambition and greed
Disregard my being
All that I need
Is a sign or an omen
Some kind of system
To relinquish this problem
My grip is loosened
Is there a sign?
Or will we keep up the pantomime
And everytime I hope, the sour taste of lime
Reminds me that you will never be mine
Is it time?
And we will keep blurring the grey lines

And we'll keep arguing in time
As if we're past our prime
Is it time?
I'm ready to die
In your eyes

To
Leah Johnson

For The Time Being

Capitulating, Mickeal Hip

For the time being, I will wallop In defeat
And suffocate under my endless questions
And you'll remind me, just by being
Of the endless manipulative illusions
I had fallen so low for
And nothing to show, for
I have fallen to your game
And fallen into my six foot grave
And you can't say my name
As if it buries you in a thick miasma of shame
And if it happens to be, you'll refrain
As if to acknowledge me brings you great pain
And my hell is your source of power
Lost within the suffocating hours
And it seems my suffering Is destined from a higher power
With each passing hour
And with the maw of infinity
Buries us for eternity

I'll grit my teeth at the agony
Of being your soul enemy
Because I'll never be your soul mate
Noting to commemorate
And I'll choke beneath the weight of your forever
Boiling up to a killing fever
Keeping all my unreadable letters
Ignoring all the papers
I leave on your desk
As if reading them is a overwhelming task
For the time being, I will relive my death
And die from holding my breath
You watched me live, now you wish for my death
And that change, still burdens my heavy head
And there's nothing left
No factory reset
What we once had
Has died, capitulate
To you, as you lacerate
At me, to manipulate
Endless, you fabricate
Some reason for me to still speculate
Received when I meet my defeat
As if I put more weight on your feet
From endlessly carrying me

But you just bury me
Beneath, all your expectation
Buried in this possession
Quelling with my obsession
Hoping to be something more than an obligation
Dismayed by your objection
And if I can hold myself against your subjugation
maybe there's hope for reunion
And I'm drowning in all my regret
As I forget
To take time for myself, to reset
Still looking to you as a prophet
Well, when the maw of this foul divinity
I'll smile and put on a facade to ignore the agony
And hope to be something more than your enemy
Choking upon my simple favour
As if it's toxic polluting vapor
Is my hell your high water?
Is everything a grab for power
And for the time being, it will submerge with my regret
And for the time being, I'll be a trophy in your closet
And you'll keep your feelings a dirty secret
And when we're together, I'll pretend

That this isn't the end
And watch how the light bends
With every back and forth
With every push and pull
With every battle on this scarred earth
I'm sentenced to a stoic jail
Never to be remembered, never to be loved
Never To be considered, to believe you were once above
To once think that this was "love"
As vultures continue to circle above
And for the time being, you will prosper from my despair
And when I need you, you'll disappear
And when I'm about to leave, you'll reappear
Penetrated by your stoic spear
Burying myself in all of the fear
That I don't belong here
And as I peer
Your getting home later
Ignoring my letters
Saying it's just better
If you discard them, one after another
And how did we become such strangers?
And how did the maw of love meet danger

And when did this indifference linger
Like we can't bear the exit of each other
And again, I choke upon the distance
And still, I fight the need for resistance
And still, I excuse your hesitance
And still, you disregard my existence
And I will relive this defeat, again
It's getting so hard to pretend
That this isn't the end
That I'm losing faith, what happened?
I told you already, I can't hold my breath forever
It's either now or fucking never
I'm desperate, not stranger
My very being is in danger
If you're seeing someone else, that's fine
I know you'll never be mine
I'm capitulated for the final time
Surrendering to these infantry lines
I'm sick of putting up a fight
Always going left, never right
Our feelings, the opposite of tight
We sit next of each other, you feverishly type
As If our love is a secret
As if you can't bear to open the closet
And let me out, you forget

I've already came out of the closet
And I'll attempt to hold my breath forever
And I'll attempt to flip the lever
I'll pretend, if it makes you feel better
Just for you, not to treat me as a stranger
Pulling myself beneath the waves of disconnect
And when the walls fall down and reset
You'll look the other way, but I know you didn't forget
Beating the weight of the agony, forget
That I exist, if that clear the abyss
Cause you can never bare the weight of two, nonetheless
I'll keep waiting for changes
And live in this-
This hell we have created
This taste that I now have hated
And I live my defeat, manipulated
And all of this, a story that's been fabricated
And I can no longer pretend, we're together
We have grown into separate strangers
Like the heart, separate chambers
And now we're met with arrest, the cells numbers
The date we met, did you forget?
Do you need a factory reset?

Who are the skeletons in your closet
You never told me that...
And I will ignore my endless question
Because if I made the decision
I'd have to do an analytics dissection
Because I have no reason
To hold my breath for you
To live for you
You remind me what the bottles of gin are for
You remind me of loves toll
Choking upon this realization
Till my guts are coughed dup
Suffocating in your regret
Forever your forbidden
Dirty tainted secret
Forever your tar trap of a burden
And when the maw of death flashes it's teeth
I'll let it drag me to sleep
Because there is nothing you have, that I need
There is no sign of relief
Stuck in your literary trap
We prepared the bags
And now, our bodies will become that
And I can no longer Ignore the fact
The you don't have my back

That the scars from the knives stack
I'm bleeding out, anemic
But I know you won't panic
Quite the opposite, manic
I can't keep pretend I'm fine
With knowing you'll never be mine
I can hold myself together
I can't keep being treated like a stranger
So finally, I surrender
Turn me into a stoic creature
There's nothing left of me
You took everything
And you won't worry
You won't show any misery
Because I'm just a tall tale, a one night story
Told to your children, a history
Buried into our veins
And yet, I remain
I'm suffocating
This is me capitulating
Maybe I deserve this
Maybe we can never seal the abyss
Maybe, there was more behind our kiss
And every truth I know, you twist
This damage can not be fixed

But still, reactions mixed
I'd put this on your desk
But my feelings are at the bottom of your "to do" list
So I'm put the dagger in my palm, and clench my fist
Watch the blood fall from my stone cold wrist
Displaying the pain you gave to me
Displaying the person turned enemy
Displaying my turbulent agony
And between antidepressants and hennessy
I'm ignoring
All of these reasons, boring
Their way into my head, I'm hurting
Finally, capitulating
You want a monster, let's seal it in this letter
I'm indifferent, will that make it better?
Which would you rather?
Cause I can be someone else, an absent father
Like mine, and you'll be like my mother
Excusing every instance of incessant behaviour
There's nothing left, nothing in our favour
This numbness walks in as a saviour
And you know... I'm done waiting
My breathe is escaping

To

Leah Johnson

Reflection

This was a really depressing time in my life. Between hospital visits and a reality that was twisted, all the warning signs of my hesitation were ignored. And this was the consequence of my opulence. I'd rather not remember this time in my life...

If I could sum it up in a saying, *rock bottom has a basement.*

But I was about to be hit with something more. A nuclear explosion of emotion that would cause such a tragedy, that I am still paying the price of it. And with that, I do acknowledge that I think of not only the next collection, but this collection from time to time. When I read each letter, I cried until my vision was an obscured muddy interpretation of my surroundings.

But all pain has a purpose. Something we can learn from. What did You learn? You'll soon find out what I learned.

About The Author

Andi Galupa is an author, Artist and musician. But all of her passions share the same need to tell a story, luckily, she has many means to express them through.

Being a trans-woman, she has been through alot in her life, giving her the experience to write the stories she does. Or to explore concepts that people usually won't look deeper into. That is her mission.

To understand the misunderstood.

This Collection

These are a collection of letters I, Michael Hip, wrote to my ex and various other people. I have grown since the beginning of that relationship, but I have a lot more growing To do. Everything has happened for a reason.

After passing the last collection, I noticed that I was a lot more numb this time around. I had given up on Any hopes of a relationship, but I kept writing letters to her, though I never showed her any.

But in my numbness was an obsession to be something more than a spectre in her existence. But sooner rather than later, that was destined to fall.

And that's how I found out why she was late All the time. So with that in mind, enjoy.

Numb

Coldly Mickeal Hip

There's a dissonance in my head
Not that you would care if I wound up dead
And I keep forgetting that we're supposedly dating
Done with your manipulating placating
But every time I think I'll surrender
The season keeps giving, like it's december
And I'm wearing a mask, hiding how I feel, october
Start of a new lesson, semptember
And what's left? What's there to be thankful? November
The doctor says numbness is normal
That with my situation, its possible
But the problem isn't only mental
It's manifested itself in a form, visceral
Like a taste that digs into the nerve endings in my tongue

Filling my body with nicotine, till the poison kills my lungs
All my insecurities are lined and leveled
Cause it's got me feeling all disheveled
Who knew us falling to this hill that's beveled
And to think that you've reveled
In my own defeat, do I even want to live?
Subjected to this thoughts, like little slits
In my mind, carved with a butcher knife
Can't find motivation to put some style in my stride
The doctor says its not my fault
Not my fault that all my feelings are in a vault
Sealed with a super glue caulk
Bought these papers in bulk
I keep trying to numb myself, but I just can't
I'm afraid my doctor is getting tired of my rants
The emotions climb to the top of the hill like ants
I can see the reality of this rampant
Emotion, ravangeing
this ruin I'm scavenging
This house is damaging
All this spite I'm packaging
Sealed with the warmest regards? False
Feeling a fading in my hearts pulse

If you don't want me. Why not pause?
Since you seem to ignore all the other words in this clause
But still, I repeat, saying "I'll do this one last time
Maybe this time, victory will be mine
And we'll retrace the border lines
And get rid of this sour tasting lime"
A symbol for our relationship
I'm lying to myself about this
Everytime I'm about to abandon ship
And jump into the oceans shape
I can't seem to find The motivation to leave you
Come and go, whenever you feel like it
What is it that I saw in you?
Nothing really, between your yelling and spit
I'm feel quite spiteful
Maybe I should be thankful
That I have someone who can't pretend to be grateful
be thankful that You showed me whats probable
and this story ends with a knife in my hand
What is it you don't understand
Can't even take care of our plot of land
Sealing and preserving this numbness into a can

And really, what's the point of being hopelessly hopeful
I mean, none of my hopes are probable
If anything, a little south of impossible
I'm struggling for clarity, it's plausible
That you're cheating on me, I suspect it
Showing later and later, text messages,
Would it be wrong if I expect it?
Between these passages of your apathy
I'm taking a lethal dose of your indifference
Again, am I your weakness?
Is that why you show such ignorance
Becoming a weird obsession
My mood keeps swinging back and forth
I keep repeating "I'm leaving henceforth"
But I Can't move forth
I'm scared, I want to move forward
These feelings- their Merging into my body
Scarring my very autonomy
An the later You show up, the more apaghetic the mentality
As if its a curse to show Be some fucking vigality
And I could say I'm pissed, but more disappointed
And your need to be above me is annoying

Not that you would acknowledge it, ignoring
But I know that you know, annoying
I transitioned from girl to man to prisoner
I'm becoming more of a spectator
No voice, just a listener
Swinging back and forth like a chandelier
And if you don't want me, just leave
Your silence is imprisoning me
Maybe I'm not what you need
Or maybe I just need some sleep
Between these lines, I read
Like I'm searching for the fine print in a deed
And the More you lead
The more I plead
But maybe that's what you want
Maybe that's what you become
What do I want?
Well first. Not to succumb
To this darkness consuming me
Eating me alive with my pleas
Guess I'm doing this "one more time"
As if I have some sort of status quo o please
It's like I stuck my hand in a wasp nest
Their eating every besides my hand, the rest
Of me is food to feed these swarming hornets

Hiding your trophies in a closet
Might as well be a casket
Line up my needs in a basket
But you never finding it
If it was Easter, you'd disregard it
Let the eggs rot
Because that's all you got
This spite that's thickening like fog
Everytime i wake up, I don't wanna be your dog
Might be a man, but I'm still your bitch
Might be a man, but it's painful to stitch
Might Be a man, but can't resist
To itch until I bleed, a crimson rich
Fluid, droppin on the floor
Done knocking On your hearts door
Done waiting for something more
Disregarding the fact that I will wait forever
more
And honestly, when the alarm goes off
I don't even wanna wake up
Got this number feelings I can't pull off
Like my nerves just burned up
And all that's left is a burnt husk
And I keep drinking hennessy and stuff
Can't remember that anymore

Can't feel anything, anymore
Couldn't fucking care anymore
I don't even live anymore
Its like- like iIm stuck in the tunnel
Heading onwards, your strings wrapping in a funnel
I see you less then a god or a colonel
And in this metaphorical tunnel
I keep walking forward but there's no signs of light
No signs or shreds of life
As if its been meticulously Crafted by a knife
Weaving in, left than right
It's like your stoic being took me over
Searching the stars for some sort of closure
Like your stabbing me when giving Me the cold shoulder
I've grown older and wiser
The idea of death disembowels me
Like suicide makes me some what free
From these emotions, enslaving and framing me
These thoughts are killing me!
Not that you would care
I'm like a child left in a fair
Left to a strangers care

Cause like my father, your never there
The second you need me, I'm here
but you don't need me, I used to fear
That in the coming year
You'd leave me right here
And our love has grown colder
Some sort of attention, I was once eager
These Pills don't numb the coldness of your shoulder
With every line, my strokes get a little bolder
Like I'm some archive in your folder
Even though winters passed, your colder
And the weight of the world is that of a boulder
And I used to scream louder
And hey, maybe I'm something to her
I dedicate this part to god, not hef
Cause I'm not gonna give her this letter
By now, I know better
Then to give her a reason, I resent her
She's showing up later and later
Like she's got a game, and if she's a player?
That would explain why she shows up later
She is always a procrastinator
With the way she acts, but anything else to her
Gets her undivided attention

As if she's got some sort of retention
Like this video is losing its pensi9n
And I'm stuck with this decision
Unrealistic and optimistic
But that's because being pessimistic
Is a foul smelling, toxic
Fume, that's becoming my automatic
Assumption
Not that she leaves me with many decisions
And she plays this fake delusion
Like I'm psychotic, lost in hallucination
But I now better than to trust her illustration
Thinking of going off my meds
Either way I suffer
And there a chance that I would be dead
If I did it without a buffer
And that's exciting
Death's maw- inviting
All care and love is exiting
And I can't shower, it's depressing
I look like the but up grease in a frier
Chunky and dripping, drooping like a flier
That was left in a thunderstorm, each shot. I'm
higher
And now I understand that I give her the power

Why would I want to shower?
When I'm getting inches per hour
There's nothing left to empower
The whiskeys got me feeling slower
Numbing myself to the pain
The doctor says I should refrain
but you, god, sent me this pain
Some sort of lesson in this picture frame
But do you really care for my pain?
The bigger lesson in this refrain?

To
Leah Johnson

Stale Prison

Tiredly, Mickeal Hip

Ladies and gentlemen, last I wrote, I was in the pale prison
Well if that had soured, now it's a stale prison
Choking On the wood in the nutritionally Depleted grains
I'm really asking the necessary questions, what do I lose or gain?
And her character is so clear
A fate that is so near
And I'm stuck inside of my own head
Wishing to just wind up dead
These letters, you never read
Left on your side on the bed
And I'm left For the coroner as you squat in the corner
Pushing me farther, pushing harder
Cause you don't have my back, that's a fact
Back to that in your silent attack

Cause my pain Gained
From your refrain that you sustain
And this picture has fractured
This deceit you nurtured
Left for the vultures
And they ignore the status quo of culture
And I'm still inside my head, waiting
And I'm playing scenes in my head, debating
Some sort of saviour, I'm fabricating
Rotting in my bed, these feelings- lacerating
And it would be nice for you to match my tone
To not leave me alone
To treat me as someone you want home
And not someone you want gone
Well, ladies and gentlemen, she'd rather not acknowledge me
Well, ladies and gentlemen, she's come to resent me
And I keep hoping For better days
Only to be met with dismay
Well, ladies and gentlemen, I'm stuck
Well, ladies and gentlemen, she doesn't give a fuck
If I died today
She would just move my body out of the way

Not to cause her any dismay
Buy she's always acting like I'm in her way
Do you even want me?
Do you ever love me?
Ladies and gentlemen, How could this be?
I guess the cost of love isn't free
Dear Leah, I've been open handed
I thought you understander
And knew I expected
Some sort of status that's respected
And every push and pull, you kill me with your resistance
Ladies and gentlemen, roles swapped, stuck in her prison
Always trapped In her calculated hesitant
I'm a rat in a cage, trying to escape the present
Wrapped under a Christmas tree and sold for spare change
Innocence Has blown away, nothing will change
Just a minor rearrangement
If you don't want me, why not split the difference
And it would be nice to hear a friendly greeting
Instead of a silent beating
Always taking me and defeating
Any hope that's got me leading

My innocence was taken put back
My innocence was attacked
And I know you don't have my back
Ladies and gentlemen, that's a fact
Every word I say, she's obliged by some social contract
The minute she can, she'll retract
This is sempiternal, lacking
a shadow of moses on the wall, stalking
Uhm, I've had enough
I try to play tough
But your promises aren't enough
To keep me around, all that masquerade stuff
And I'm hardly outside my head, still
I've fallen into a crimson sickness, ill
And you could destroy me with will
This is something that can't be treated with a pill
And you were once, the only person I trusted
But that door as rusted
And every action is encrusted
What's there left? You cannot be trusted
Your turning me down, burying me under ground
Got me hopelessly heart bound
And within your silence and inaction, I found
That this is a battleground

And it's not that I'm lonely that bothers me
It's the fact you made me the enemy
And all of the created agony
But I know, oh how I know
That this is all a show
Waiting for the storm to clear the snow
But you'll still stand, stone cold
What's left? What's the weight?
What did we feel? A taste so faint
It was lost in the sour taint
Of our rotting decay
And I know you'll never read this
As if to do so would mean to acknowledge this abyss
This creatures been evolving, metamorphosis
And I'm hardly surviving this reality Twist
And I'm left in the corner, still
Pushing for something, still
enslaved to you, still
Lying to myself that everything is okay, still
A rat in a cage
Destined to become enraged
And we sink into flames
This fantasy we portrayed
Has soured and sautéed

This garden we once made
Is now decayed
And it would be nice, to know if you fucking care
To know that if I was a die, you would dare
To fucking care
I'm Angry, this spite i have to bare
Into the nerve endings in my teeth
Not meeting any of my basic needs
Between this Poison encrusted lines you read
Is the spite you have now taken to breed
And I guess I don't understand, where have you been?
Why don't you just tell me where you been?
Is there a burden to answer that question
As your cheeks are flushing, the silence is crushing
I feel intangible, dissociated from reality
Lost in this fake, extravagant formality
I'm starting to notice similar themalities
Still waiting for you to orbit back to me
Again, I keep pushing, but you never pull
As if our love has become so dull
When did your heart Become null?
Just waiting for this spite to cool
But the fire keeps raging, enslaving

Can't keep isolating and debating
Whether you indifference is making
Me want to reconnect
To your desolation
It's become less love and more fascination
A belief that some where, there's morality
That you have a different mentality
Towards me, vitality
But no, that's no reality
Cause I'm hardly thinking, anymore
I can't even bare to walk out the door
All of this, I didn't ask for
I didn't know this was in store
Ladies and gentlemen, what would you do?
Ladies and gentlemen, did this happen to you?
Spill your guts, make it true!
Or do you just sink into the ocean blue
What's left to gain but shame?
Do you even care for my name?
Does acknowledging me cause you pain?
Is there no fucks that you can refrain to remain
Splintered and fractured
I have a suspicious Feeling I nurtured
This hulking vulture
Still waiting for you to read my lecture-

Is that what it is? A burden?
A problem that You'd rather ignore, ghen
Solve it with some sort of caring system
And when you with someone, you shouldn't feel ashamed
You should feel as if they care And lvoe to say your name
That your the life force pumping in their veins
And not some picture hanging by gold frames
What status do I give you? What ambition fools you?
What's lie and what's true? Wanna know what I saw in you?
Well, whatever I saw in you, I now know isn't true
And I'm done excusing every action made by you?
You gave my back, cause your always down to stab
Dig your knives in with a quick emotionless jab
But once I call it out, to the hills you ran
As if you want to hide the blood on your hands
Every time you say you can, but you can't
Always ignoring my rants
Now I know, care? You can't

Now these feelings rampant
Up to a boiling point
And for a while, I've been your toy
Grown up, man from boy
That you just plant like soy
Taking up the water
Draining the clouds in its shower
My hell is your higher power
And you won't stop, getting highef and higher
Till you crumble upon the sun
and icarus, you have nowhere to run
What is done is done
Now we sit, watching you run
Chasing some sort of dream
Like you need a change of the scene
And I always thought this is how things have been
You didn't see what I had seen
Your losing your grip on me
Soon, I'll wriggle my way free
And I've been dreaming of you leaving me
So I had an excuse, to finally be free
But you keep me around, a trophy
Yet wage war, enemy
Causing this endless agony
Cause You don't wanna let realty

Finally set in
I'm at wit ends
And ignorantly, you pretend
The same cycle, again and again

To
Anyone Who Cares

Emerging

Realizing, Mickeal Hip

We dive head first, into the water, we submerge
Ignoring the problems that had emerged
Cursing the roses for its thorn
Between these pages, I'm torn
Are we close to an end?
Are you sick in your stomach pretending?
Because I am the fire that once burned
Before your face churned and your back turn
Go ahead and leave, I've come to peace
Go ahead and leave, leave me in pieces
Go ahead and leave, it's time to renew this lease
Go ahead ahead leave, offer me this final release
And your poison, infiltrated
Now I see, your takeover was calculated
You predicted How I capitulated
And once you had me in your prison, you retracted
Cause you knew, I would surrender

Came in as a saviour
Left like a vapour
Your actions show through behaviour
Go ahead and leave, release your maw
Go ahead and leave, crimson dripping from your jaw
Go ahead and leave, pretend you god and you can ignore law
Go ahead and leave, at the notice of a ravens caw
And will every push and pull
I'm left in the blistering cold
Your strokes, once bold
Now growing so old
Crumbling to your story told
Through teeth and bullet holes
Swallowing our pride and future, whole
Pulled to the depths, beneath the beast's Hull
And you can pretend I won't alchemize
but now I'm fully realized
This threat, you could have nuetralized
Leave or stay, you decide
Come closer, Let me see your ego shine through
Like every decision you make, comes from a bureau
Well, finally I've pushed through

I'm done waiting at the ravens que
Go ahead and leave, I'll pack the bags
Go ahead and leave, as I light up a fag
That's okay with me
You absence will leave me free
To finally just be
Even for a moment, happy
You'll still rush into battle
You'll still make enemies
But, you lost this battle
And I have no more pleasantries
There's nothing left in this masquerade
So let the curtain close fade
But I know that you won't
Care for me, we established, you don't
Admit your treating me so below
Admit it, you won't
Cause you don't want to acknowledge
The reality of this hemorrhage
And the causation of this damage
Your still under the spell of this voyage
I'm just some burden, a package
And if I get damaged
That's fine, we'll still voyage
Cause you'll still manage- without

So go ahead and leave, the harm you've done to me
So go ahead and leave, release your arms from holding me
So go ahead and leave, bells and alarms, Free me
Go ahead and leave, sail away frombme
Because my issues are nano
You won't acknowledge them, no!
I'm carbon in a cartridge
Burst fire, hitting with every package
Mixing It up in porridge
Well, I'm done waiting for my meal, done being a servant
Sick of being treated as a nuisance
I wish I had listened to the hesitation
Now I see that within it is a lesson
Cause now, in your manipulation
You keep threatening to leave, go ahead
Keep threatening to leave, well go ahead
Keep threatening this and that, well go ahead
Your spineless, show different, go ahead
Your not a savior
You pay the expenses for your power
Welding your dagger
Blood on your rapier

Crimson a paint, you shower
This battle, for power
I'm letting you have the vapor
Because if I can't have love, you can't have the power
You keep me under your thumb
To keep me so numb
Playing me, I'm not dumb
Even if there's some rum
In my lungs
I see the cracks In your tongue
Fissures and pressured, these ropes, you had me hung
Your Castles And thrown is the equivalent to dung
So go ahead and leave, show some spine
Go ahead and leave, you whege never mine
Keep waging war, read the past line
Your not and never will be mine
And I'm done trying to submerge
And done waiting for you to emerge
Responsible for all this pain and hurt
As if to love me is nine to five work
And maybe someday, you'll fully realize
What I had saw in those eyes

And maybe, when you eventually realize
It won't hurt you like It hurt me when it died
So come on, your not who you where
It's like we were never there
Awoke the sleeping bare
Now it's teeth sink In here
Again, leave, if you so please
Again, leave, your no queen
Again, leave, there's other bees
Again, leave, because maybe you don't deserve me
And we can keep up this battle
I'll play dirty, there's my tattle
Show my fangs, hear my rattle
I'm done being your paddle
Cause every day with you is a struggle
There's no end to this tunnel
Keep seeing like a funnel
I'm a season colonel
We aren't lovers, we're enemies
Separate, converging realities
Emerging, fatalities
Never submerging into your pleasantries
And I've got plans for your manipulations
Backup incase of complications

There's no confusion
Shakespeare translation
Thee will me dashed upon thine metal Door
Forevermore, a enslaving power whore
Pretending to be some sort of saviour
Heathen grasping at the vapour for power
Set my mind free and leave me behind
This house you leave me, confined
You robbed me blind
Well I can see the grey line
Never meant to be mine
More concerned with a bottom line
This endless charade we pantomime
Sucking the venom out of the lime
Go ahead and leave, gratefully
Go ahead and leave, gracefully
Done playing into your games
Done with the endless names
Done with this exponential pain
There's nothing left for either of us to gain
But still you take, take, take
Every spontaneous moment I'm awake
But you can't have me, if I don't participate
I just have to hunker down, and concentrate
And who am I? You didn't care to know

Tell me who I am, let it go to show
That you never dare to Know
The only thing you thought I was, was slow
It's time for us to go
To finally end this cycle and say no
So please go and leave
Please, give me that relief
Cause no longer do you have my belief
I said my part, now leave
Your strings are no longer around
I fly as a bird, burden free
Done excusing thee
I'll diss thine in old speak
You've mistaken me for weak
Not that you would let your sentiment leak
Onto the concrete floor, my pain peaked
And when you showed me release
I realized you could not be pleased
I got up and off my knees
Wielded my sword and held up my word
Go and leave, your not welcome here
Go and leave, I do not fear
Your retaliation
It's another verbal manipulation
Go ahead and leave, this is not a plea

Go ahead and leave, you are no quren
You left me with confusion
Now I'll leave you with this translation
I got spite for your dances
Lost in your literary cadence
A stimulating nutrition
Depleting My senses
We are now caught in conflagration
Take the mask off, the wolf behind the fascination
Sentencing our love to damnation
Leaving is our only salvation
And for the moment of clarity I have
You treat me less than half
That's a respect, I must have
Or I will leave you in half
This is no threat, it's a promise
Get off these premises
I've come to my senses
This is a final consensus
Leave, there's no option
Leave, clear the confusion
Leave, this translation
Final decision
It's too late to change
Don't try to rearrange

Placate, arrange
Some sort of finale to this play
Well, not today
Now get out of my way
Sorry if it causes you dismay
Now that I can anyway
And this spite builded up every day
Done of being thrown to the wolves
There's no hope to resolve
By morning, when sun sets
I'll be gone, You'll be lucky to get
Some sort goodbye
And I am the fire in the eyes
Of destiny, you indifference, A fabricated tragedy
I'm done living in two separate realities
There's nothing left
Bug to close the book
Go ahead and leave
I don't need to give this another look

To
Leah Johnson

Blood And Fury

Spitefully, Mickeal Hip

You say that you forgive
But There's no more fucks to give
I am a fire, I am the spirit
So instigate, cause this spirit
Will flow eternal
Say that this is all mental
But you made it impossible
You knew this would be probable
Are you exhausted, like your buried
In all of this blood and fury
Your a royal purple
And I'm the red in the outer circle
of your prison
Sick of being your victim
Your indifference, that Was the problem
The red tape in your eternal system
And if this is what you truly believe
That I am the One who took leave
Like I'm just looking for release

If that's what you believe
That that tis what you will receive
So drop it on me
Cause you Won't, Have me again
And I won't, capitulate
And you won't, have to pretend
That You don't fabricate
And you can't resist the verbal violence
You can resist but to be insulated In ignorance
As if a child, striking back in defiance
You are no longer my reliance
And that's when you dropped it on me
That you were cheating on me
That's why you were late, cheating on me
Thats when I screamed "get the fuck away from me!"
And you left without a word
The crumbling of this world
All my feelings were hurled
As it's foul vines twirled
It seems this was a fire, and I was dry to the bone
And now, finally and officially alone
Instigating the walls of this Home
To the aching pain in my bones
Knowing, you'll never come back

Knowing, the truth of the fact
Knowing, that this is an attack
I can never retract
I was exhausted from the blood and fury
And I attempted To bury
This silence, with the fire and fury
Of a thousand suns, you left in a hurry
And I was left here, contemplating
Debating and relating
Back to you indifference, complication
Calculating and waiting
If All of this is to be believed
Then I know why you refused
To love me, and I had excused
You, ignoring the rules, excused
All of the nights, alone
All of the Shallowness in this home
I swam up to the surface
Revoking a sense of lost purpose
And if that's all to believe
Then it's better that you leave
I packed up your things
Opened the window and flinged
Them onto the green lawn
Right at the Crack of dawn

I was in shock and awe
Finally released from your maw
Your silence consumed me
Buy within that truth was a violence, harming me
The debt that I owe?
The Apology I owe?
To you, I owe
Write it out in a text but I owe
You nothing
You gave me nothing
And now, I see something
Something, if anything
I let a wolf into my home
I let you penetrate the marrow in my bones
I won't let that happen again
I won't pretend
It stings and hurts to the nerve'S ends
Your sickness, a pathogen
Your presence, equivalent to an assassin
And all that could have been
Brings me a little lower, all that we Could have been
I see, I see it clearly now
That's not how it would go down

And in this hopeful optimism, I found
And founding ground
A new temple To build
Something new has curled
Around my neck, sitting on my queen sized bed
You might as well be dead
But I can't distract myself from this pain in my head
And the way you lead me with your play Of pretend
And you can remember, when we met
You said, you would never forget
And that you would never regret
And now, we can never reset
this fire rages on
The damage has been done
Blow me away, like a gun
Keep your ammo, I'll keep on the run
Scarlet mixing with the ultraviolet
This mental warfare, verbal Violence
And I'll keep myself in a well balanced silence
Glad to Be done with your indiffegence
But the revelation Still stings
And still, I'm coming to terms with things
The taste lingers, queen and king

Dethroned, over such petty things
I was such a stranger
And you where a danger
Your a gas grenade With the way you linger
I'm disappointed it took me so long to figure
Out who you where, but now it hurts
And now, I gotta put in the work
Go into the fray, lurch
Into Gotham From my bats perch
Now is the time to become a man
Cause I'm coming to terms, doing what I can
Revolving in a circle like, ceiling fan
You eat up my happiness, but you ran
And finally, towards life, I feel like I actually can
You came back, and I let you in
You tried your semantics, you began
But I shut you down, found my peace within
You took your stuff And Ran
In a way, I felt this pain in my chest
But maybe it will go away when I go to rest
Just a passing cloud, A test
Cause I know in the end, it's for the best
And as the days progress
And as my life resets
I pretend, but I can not forget

Because if I did, I would regress
Back Into the maw of some other beast
A pray For the predator to eat
Letting you become my souls defeat
I'm standing, Off my knees, on my two feet
We're not going back to blood and fury
So grab the shovel, and bury
All your disdain with the past
Out! With this shadow you forever cast
Replaying fiction of a ongoing past
How we went back and forth
Forever moving backwards
Cause every step forward
Was eternally mirrored
Reflected off your glass eyes
How our love met its demise
When I finally grew wise
To your endless lies
I suppose I should feel triumphant
But there's a weight on my chest, like an elephant
Some sort of overwhelming shadow of malevolence
I look towards the future, expecting to feel benevolence
But this boiling could ran is churning

I try to keep from turning
But these curiosities burning
I still have your social media, prodding
This overwhelming insecurity
That this is something I can not bury
Where the light meets the tree lines fur6
I'm hiding in the shadows of our dead history
But the past never dies
As Long as it's in your head, it never dies
No matter how much lead, it never dies
No matter what, it never dies
Never capitulating, always lacerating
Done with your fabricating
Overcoming your manipulating
But there's this feeling, that I am regressing
I want to go back, but I know that means death
But I give this curiosity the weight of my breath
Looking for some shadows to sit down and rest
This heavy weight in my stone like chest
And each time we battled, it's blood and fury
Left me exhausted, leaving in a hurry
These scars, I will forever carry
This dawn setting over This parry
And in a way, I miss that
It's weird, how after the fact

You leave this taste with the knife in my back
That, I can not ignore that
As the knife Carves into my bones
And the difference between us, is hidden in the fact that I'm alone
And you drifted off and got your own home
I know I should feel happy, but this painful stinging in my bones
Is getting to me, I'm lonely
And for some reason, I'm ready
To let you back into my reality
But I know the twisted tongue of apology
And the fictitious twists of Your masquerading fantasy
It's like cutting you Out was a tragedy
And I hate that I look at it as a travesty
I hate how it still hurts me
And I can't help but to look
Upon Instagram and Facebook
Stalking me like the hunter in your blood
Hiding behind the structure's of wood
That reach toward the sky
And obscure my eyes
And in a way, I still believe your lies
But there Just that, lies

And every moment of this silence
Exposes you backhanded violence
In a way, I still expect repentance
Guess I'm stuck in recession
Cut you out, but I'm still obsessed
In a way, kind of possessed
Caught you, rephrased
Your daggers for some other person, what did I expect
Did I ever deserve your lack of respect?
I know this is for the best
I know, but again, my hearts bleeding out of my chest
And like a cloud sprinkling Snow
The finale of our show
Pantomiming is all you know
But in the same breath, your all that you know
I kicked you out
But now, I am entertaining the doubt
This silence, screams so loud
You go on, looking for other trout
Why Do I still believe
That your selfishness shelters Me?
What should I beleive?
That is was a curse to let you leave

This fire is extinguished
A taste, Rotten and distinctive
What is this from your perspective
Did you look at me, respectively?
I'm still lonely

To
Leah Johnson

Emotional Blackout

Angrily, Mickeal Hip

Still waiting, for your consideration
Your understanding and fascination
Leaving me in the middle of destitution
Your very being scars humanity
I hate the fact we share a reality
Turn, back to the fantasy
And yet, I persistent formality
Now I know evil have a face
Now I know That you take its place
Now I Know, your evils face
Now I Know, emotional blackout has taken its place
Return, to the ashes from whence you came
Burn, This shallow husk I became
Needing a medical equalizer
Equivalent to a horse tranquilizer
Now I know, I am wiser
You are sufferings creator

And to this new host you infect with your pathogen
To become a silent and deadly Assassin
Hiding the Truth in your calculated Confession
Because ambition is your only fixation
You are the Flies and the trash heap
You see so you can selfishly Reap
I don't know why I still weep
Your no god, just another symptom of the weak
Sense of self I have
Cut and halved
Thinking about you? I can't
Falling upon your spike trap
The endless fascination
Drugged by my opaque obsession
Genetically, a mental separation
Now you have go, along with your possession
Now I see, your evils face
Now I see, the devils in place
Now I see, you Will keep up the pace
As if life is an endless race
You'll fill your cup, but it's never enough
Faking your mental muscles, never enough
Appearing strong and tough
But that's just a ideal though

You tangle yourself with the flames
You keep your partners like picture frames
You endlessly come up with games
Hiding behind your false affectionate names
Fire, is on the horizon
You Were a vulture, resting upon carrion
Now, you have revealed your face
Taking true evils place
To run amok among the universes pace
I hate that I still can remember your face
Everything falls upon its knees
You'll go on, bloody queen
Building your throne off Of the Backs of other bees
Always exploiting to full your needs
Endlessly, you'll feed
Infinitely, gaining greed
Finishing, upon your wicked steeds
You've done this deed
Your a recreant
Even hungry after the meal, you finish it
And keep me as a hidden secret
And now I see what your status meant, It is complicated
Cause once you keep up a lie

You have to be able to say it infront of eyes
And hope to God the truth Doesn't die
Harvesting the sustaining rye
Leaving barren, These fields, your harming
Harvesting, your greed, subtly Alarming
This personal, your miming
Like your a hacker, data mining
Well I'm a corrupted software
Watch the seams Fall apart and tear
Wishing for you to feel an ounce of my fear
Because, I know the face behind the Mask you wear
But yet I'm still Scared
From this burden I once bared
Left in dilation
Your very being is still my obsession
Even though you Left, this possession
All these feelings, leaving a taste of confusion
Could it be out Society
That Feeds your twisted reality
Your strings attached to pleasantries
So you can throw your status away like toiletries
And in this trash heap, your throne lays
Everyone but you pays
And you celebrate your growth each day

Acting like this is somewhat fucking okay
You brought the kerosene, now lite it
Nothing left, finish it
You planted the sow, now Reap it
Nothing left, despite that, you believe it
Take your grip, and release it
Purposeful, Another host, deceive it
Sucking out the life from a once happy being
Make them turn, leave them bleeding
Nothing left, threatening
Your indifference with the scars your leaving
Desperation, the nature Of our species
Obsession, the language of our reality
Copulation, birthing your fantasy
Population, caught In this repeating tragedy
Does it feel deceitful, to not show your face
Does it feel unlawful, how you achieved your fame
Does it seem unjust, how you keep your hosts in place
Parasitic, until they bled dry. Then you replace
Rotting and decayed
This debt, you never payed
Entire lives, laid
Completely in waste, left in a firey Daze

Overcoming the haze
Like your burning the sustaining maize
Your a fire and a parasite
Sparking conflagration, parasite
Destroying everyone's lives
Sustaining of the death of others, parasite
Now take your grip, and release it
My life, you Disintegrate
All my reasons, incinerate
Take someone else's life, and believe it
Why is, it in your absence
The deafening dissonants of silence
Portrays this portrait of violence
No longer by your side, yet compliant
Cause now I know, I was destined to be replace
Cause no I know, my life has be defaced
And your ambition slightly delayed
This tale, will be replayed
Turn, into the ashes that you Really are
Return, back from hell where you came
Burn, show the true person you are
Return, back from the devilish womb you came
If I was just ta host
If I was just a trophy, to gloat
Then why did you care if I stayed afloat

When I was a asset, you, the "goat"
Fits well, the way you eat and eat
The way you Take and take
The way you bring grief
With every breath you take
Your not a human, not deserving of humanity
Your a devil, a plague on humanity
And truthfully, that's the fucking reality
Everything collapses, what a "tragedy"
You lit the fire, fucking finish it
You can't retire, fucking finish it
Emotional blackout, disintegrate
All your efforts, subject to concentrate
This act we replicate
This story, you made to complicate
It's funny, how who you love become who you hate
This is the impression you make
It's said that someone could Create
Such. Creature, capable of hate
Masking all the intentions
Too keep away the hosts attention
To eventually black out the Emotion
Ignoring the very actions notion
Place your innocent

Show your indifference
Subject to your ambition
Fed off your narcissism
Devoid Of any feeling
Every situation, your dealing
The story, your complicating
Destroyed in your endless Harvesting
There's nothing left to sustain your existence
This ambition is your strength and weaknesses
And until you can stop all resistance
You'll keep up your indifference
Your A parasite
Requesting other people compensate
For everything you selfishly take
And all the false beliefs you make
How could I love someone I now hate
Destined to not replicate
This weight, you substantiate
No longer can you delay
You must feed until the end of your days
Everything to you is a play
And as the hosts skin decays
You'll still make them pay
I'm ashamed you exist on this side of flesh
Peel away the beast behind the death

My sanity, lost within a single breath
Ripening the herd for a Meal, falsely called fresh
I see it, between the blood and flesh in your teeth
Suffocating beneath your Greed
And yet, I am not free
Still, eternally enslaved to thee
Your teeth, are fake
Just like the love you make
Manufactured with calculated hate
As if to show the capricious emotion you make
Absorbing the host for your own vitality
Because nothing is too much, that's the mentality
Never being showing You, because in reality
You are scared to show The devil making the tragedy
Burn, foul Demon of worship
Burn, this face of factitious
Burn, Ambition is your weakness
Burn, cursed is your existence
Don't you see, you and evil share a place
Don't you see, you share the same face
Ruination, Keep it the pace
Don't you see, don't you see the relation?
Leaving so called "Partners" in devastation
Your a parasite, akin to infestation

This hosts, perilous in Your invasion
With the lies of your emotion
This is your nature
As if two faces is the culture
Your feed off the carcass of love like a vulture
Like a mother who manipulates her nurture
Painting a devilish caricature
Leah, the hosts destroyer
Leah, hopes annihilator
Leah, the parasitic creature
Your indiffered, not a bug, just a feature

To

The Parasite

An Apology In Ink

Apologetically, Mickeal Hip

My apologies, Emoticones Weight took my strength
And let me know, if I Made any difference
Maybe there was a reason for your hesitance
Maybe, there was something behind your silence
And all of it sacred violence
Maybe, I plagued your existence
Maybe I was your weakness
And maybe I'm the reason we sunk into the ocean
Maybe we were just going through the motions
And I'd give anything to spare the difference
And show you my new temperament
To not live with this eternal punishment
My anger and it's consequence
Buy worry not
The battles tie themselves like knots
And my offenses can not
Keep up with the piling lot

And I'd give anything, to have you sleep a next of me
To understand that You still love me
To understand the indifference with certainty
Maybe I just can't come to terms with reality
My blood is running cold
And I see, I have not grown old
But simply detailed in Bold
Stroke, pulled
From the arms of the heavens
For us heathens
And I'm sinking
Choking and heaving
I guess the cycle is grieving
I guess I'm harvesting, reaping
While I remain here, weeping
Looking at the water below, waiting, leaping
Into the depths below
This feeling is not unknown
And as I stare out the window
I'd give anything just to know
If you feel something for me
Curiously, how you can be
Now that you're Without me
And your social medias, you look so happy

Maybe you were thinking of leaving
Maybe there's something behind my weeping
Between these lines, I'm reading
My obituary, deathly ill in your leaving
And are you still sowing and reaping?
And I'm feeling, the emptiness In the bed
The weight pulling me, what's dead is dead
And why do I let it get to my head?
Why can't I just sleep in this bed?
Why can't I go back to being innocent
Back to when I was hesitant
I should have been more resistant
Cause now, the burden of the punishment
Is crushing
My feelings ,gushing
The dam, flushing
And I'm submerging, Descending
I'd give anyyhing, fucking anything
To know, that to you, I meant something
Just about anything
To not Feel like nothing
This wrists healed, but I'm still bleeding
And I know you'll never be reading
These letters, I continue writing
Wanting to give up the fighting

And give into my descending
Are you still set on ascending?
Without me, are you transcending
My conscious, rescinding
Is it normal, to be regretting
The decisions, forgetting
What lead to them?
The unaddressed Problems
And the unlearned lessons
Am I obsessed with your systems?
Your strings and control
Though gone, Still have control
Burning my veins like petrol
I'd give anything to null
This sinking feeling, to pull
You back
And even in this Aftermath
Ignoring all the facts
And how they overwhelmingly stack...
I'm crawling, like I have missing limbs
Paying any token, while your sleeping
I'm restlessly weeping
And in all of this walloping
And maybe I'm in For rebounding
Can't quite entertain dating

And in moments like this, I should start grounding
But with Every shot I'm downing
In my grief, I'm drowning
And this feeling, and your lack of frowning
Are you, too, drowning?
Our love, decayed and browning
My defenses have lost in this cascading
Mountain, feeling this receding
Anguish, proceeding
Without you, Regretting
Every moment of silence
Replacing your violence
With my own malevolence
Knowing your living In benevolence
It's like, staring through the cracks in a fence
Watching your life, my Purposeless existence
How could you, after all this time, still be my weakness
My eternal obsession
And I'm still your puppet
Your regret
Hidden in your closet
Your drained deposit
Which Your collected

And neglected
I'd give my life
Just to know if I caused you strife
I'd give any sacrifice
To know, if My life
Meant anything to you
To know, if any of your feelings where true
And do you, too
Feel this descending blue
Like the island is drowning In the ocean
Like, like this lack of emotion
Sets the notion
That something deep was in motion
But worry not, I'd forgive you
Not that you worry at all
But worry not, it's all true
Not that You feel that at all
But worry not, I'd sink into those eyes, like the ocean blue
Not that you would fall
Into that cascading ocean blue
And this apology in ink
This moment, missing in the blink
Of my eyes, brought to the blink
Draining in the bathroom Sink

Pulling all of my feelings
Puking, all of these feelings
Brandishing Hennessey
I can't keep hoping on fantasies
And the weight of these tragedies
And their weight and travesties
Do you miss me at all?
How can you stand tall?
Do you fucking feel at all?
Cause I can't even feel, at all
Numb to it all, but that's a lie
Cause somewhere between my bloodshot eyes
Somewhere, where oceans collide
That place, where our love died
I thought I had overcome The yide
I guess I lied
I thought I finally realized
But I lost that vision in the tide
And when did I get this spit
Like a moving sprite
And with the fading night
And the forthcoming light
Worry not, our blessing amount
to something greater than ourselves
Worry not, as I scream so loud

But If nothing else
You won't worry at all
You'll still stand so tall
To neverless fall
And with the roosters call
You'll awake
And I'll steel ache
Never asleep, never awake
Somewhere between this Painful paint
The picture we disintegrate
Our house, well mine now, i with to incinerate
Just to see it go up in flames
To Take this numbness, and run away
To know that this is like a passing day
To just feel an ounce Of "okay"
What every that is anyways
I'm giving anything, just to feel something
And if my life just amounts to nothing
Then let me know, let me kiss the ring
Let me feel just something
How can you just forget Me in a blink
And now I'm on the brink
To know, I was once your king
And now, to you, I am nothing
Just A void

And I can not avoid
Looking at your social media, like a Polaroid
I can't stop looking at the picture, somewhat annoyed
To know you can just smile
To know. That even After a short while
You can move on, but that was your style
To know, that after a short while
You'll abandoned the sinking ship
Forget that you even had a relationship
How can I still find a way to worship
Stuck in this dissonance
Something oh so resonant
Playing this endless symphony
This hellish reality
You'll Be my fatality
You've become my only Medalitt
Of suffering
Your not even buffering
Not even an Ounce of suffering
Not even an ounce of this, lingering
This weight in my chest
This weight, like breasts
Hanging me down, is this a test?
Is this what I should expect?

For the rest of my days
To relive this endless play
To never sleep, to always drink away
My sorrows, to run away
From everything
Because nothing
Is what it used to be
Do you even think of me?
Do you even acknowledge Me?
When asked, what do you tell them about me?
"Just a passing moment
Just a mountainous Burden
Just Capulet
Opposing a Montague, a capulets
The exact opposite Of you"
And I suppose that could be true
And I suppose, I'm Still obsessed with you...

To
Leah Johnson

Hollow

Diplomatically, Mickeal Hip

Uhm- I flip switch quick
Who could have seen the bottom I'd hit
Tumbling among the fallen leaves and twigs
Getting dirty with the pigs
I'm on a different level of anguish
This fire you left, I have to extinguish
Listening at the spite in your language
I try to keep my head above it
How can you come back like that
Like you Never been through that
But thats apart of you twisting of facts
And it's immaculate
How your rising when I collapse
Smoking up cigarettes, I relapse
Everythings coming outside, prolapse
I'm hanging By my spilled guts, a lapse
In my judgement and senses
I was justified in my census

But I can't ignore this full on attack, penance
To what I saw in You, grappling, violently, with the silence
I guess I wasn't Smart enough
I guess I wasn't tough enough
How do you keep your head up?
Like, how can you stride and stuff?
Maybe I didn't mean anything
Like I'm nothing
Your somebody else, no- something else
I'm bary Holding onto myself
And maybe I should wait for god to strike you down
Is it sadistic that I just wanna see you frown?
See you crumble To the Ground
Like you've finally found
The hurt you bury beneath your accomplishments
And in all your insulation Ignorance
Misunderstanding The purpose of punishment
Cause you misunderstand what the consequence
Is- maybe I'm out of my mind
Maybe I should just leave this behind
Why, After All this time
I still try to confide

In you, it's all true
What that shows about you
It's all true
My apology, impromptu
It's a fiction, a book written
With hopeful diction, A fixed addiction
I'm withdrawal, still addicted
Yet I predicted it! Collected it!
I stare in the mirror, I see this hole you left
Like you stole my heart in literary theft
And nothing is going to heal that
That's a fucking Fact!
I just want you to tell me if I was the problem?
And if there's a god, tell me the lesson
What keeps me tied to your system
This hope that I'm holdin'
It's disappearing
As I'm clearing
My mind, peering
Past the mirror, peering
Into my lonely soul
Worn out, My lonely soul
Can't even look at the Cereal in my bowl
Cause it feels like I'm full
But it's deplete, null and void

All these realizations I try to avoid
And the more I entertain them, the more annoyed
I become, like literary soldiers have been deployed
How could I have Become a toy?
Another bait and switch, a ploy
From girl to boy
And yet, It Still annoys
My very soul, down to its venomous petrol
I stare at this full bowl
But I can't ever fill my feeling of null
Taking all these thoughts, pull
On my heart strings, cut out and starved
My very appetite, harmed
My senses, somewhat alarmed
Your absence, carved
From the heavens And hell
A drought succumbing This well
I feel this rain, this storm, as it pelts
My sense, a full on salt, it pelts, pelts
Until I'm broken down and eroded
Until I'm lost, never found, proliferated
In The form of some on else, perforated
You'll rip em apart till their something you can harvest

And I almost think of writing to you
My friend says "do what you gotta do"
What do I gotta do to convince you
To Come back, to do it impromptu
But in the same breath, I fucking hate you now
You fucking disgrace, and how
Could such a vile trash bag of a human being
Existed here and now, always lying
To everyone they exploit
For their own Purpose, of which they anoint
Back To my point
I guess I have no point
I'm Just writing, cause me and this paper where once similar
Without purpose, blank, but once your introduced, it's familiar
And you can be reintroduced, it's for a better
That you stay away, but I still wish for a ladder
To reach you in the sky
How can You survive off of lies
Do you see the tears in my eyes
I believe in you, I realized
You don't deserve my belief
You don't deserve this release
But still, I write, for my own relief

Why can't I just overcome this belief
That I owe you some debt
Like, somehow, your answer will make me content
To you, I was met with contempt
I said what I meant
Not that you would know
Not that you would care
If you did, you wouldn't show
You would dare
I'm feeling hollow
Always dreading tomorrow
How could you leave me with this sorrow?
All my emotions, you Stole, not borrowed
Cause you Won't return them
Just burn them
Twist and churn them
Into some new problem
That you can manufacture
This hanging creature
You'll make it your newest Feature
I worshipped you like a preacher
Yout somebody else, you smiled
But thats in your condescending style
Descending, and after a while

I saw you and Your style
And I write to you cause it's escape
Though, these feelings continue to cascade
As you find someone else to masquerade
No matter what, I still try to placate
As you find new people to build and make
To create
And once they go on a date
You Concentrate
Taking over them, obsession
Cause all they are, is a possession
I'm angry at myself, if nothing else
How i still love you, when I can't love myself
I'm stressed out, I Don't love myself
How could I love anyone else?
Why do I still hope?
You kicked the chair, tied The rope
And now I See, misanthrope
Between sad and angry, I hope
That if God's punishing you, it comes soon
Yet with you, I still Swoon
Got me trapped in this cocoon
Never to escape, wild like a raccoon
Spitting and hissing While your still kissing

What am I missing, Other then you, all these reasons, Listing
Take me down in some battle, fishing
For some sort of reason, fisting
Some superficial cure
This is a test right? I have to endure
Watch my life incinerate and burn
These feelings, I still lure
I'm not hollow enough
I'm not tough enough
I can't wake up
Still asleep, Drowsy and Stuff
Can't even this straight
Can't give a solid reason to this hate
In on letter, I love you
In the other, my anger Springs impromotu
Maybe I gotta dig a little deeper
Find if the feelings steeper
Find paper that's cheaper
Might take a month to a year
But there's something here
I can't admit it, I fear
And to you, It's just mere
Coincidence That you leered
Me over with your bait

This story, you create
I can't escape
Can't placate
But wait, I keep writing
I keep fighting
These bridges, lighting
The sky, tightening
The noose around my neck
Wrong side, I apologize
Maybe I should have realized
This would be dramatized
And I keep writing, tranquilized
Like I'm gonna push these words into your skull
Scar the ships hull
Fill the void, can't null
Made with consonants and vowels
My retribution written in verbal translation
Apparently, I wasn't smart enough, translation
I couldn't See through the conflagration
Cause I'm just another project, accomplishment
A trophy on your shelf
And to think I felt
That You understood me, trophy Case
Evil with a feminine face
I'll be the mirror, I'll show you what we see

Your a disgrace, a plague on me
And I'm digging my water out to be free
But You still control me
I got a problem, and this problems
Got a whole system
To keeping me in it
Like the meaning behind this is hidden
It's right up in your face, I hate you
But even that is only half true
There's No getting to you
Breaking through
The glass cage, enslaved
To this dream, Cascade
to a crescendo, escape
From this enraged flame
And if I showed this to you, you'd act surprised
Like you were never just as wise
Well, fuck, surprise!
Here's How I feel inside
Fending for your cruelty
Cooking this up, fermenting like a brewery
Letting these feelings fester up, unruly
My sense of morality
I'll fill this void with hennessy
Cause I'm done living a fantasy

But in reality
We know I can't sustain that tragedy
Cause everytime I move forward and move on
I'm crippled by fates gun
And what's done is done
But I can't help but run
From these emotions
It was your notion
That everything set In motion
Doesn't matter, that's the notion
I could write you a thousand times
Write all these feelings of mine
But you wouldn't Even read the first line
Cause you can't ever care about whats mine
Digging deeper within myself
Trying to find something else
Like you, living in this house
It's empty without you, I'm mouse
In a huge labrinth
All my tears dripping down like a sink
And days move on in a blink
How could you bring me to the brink?

To
Leah Johnson

Iceberg

Still, Mickeal Hip

Staring at the eyes of the beast
While I sit Down for the Thanksgiving feast
I haven't written for a while, you went east
And I guess I just can't give myself the treat
Of letting go, staring into the eyes
What's between this twists and turns, these lies
It's strange, your miles away, and between
dwindling mental supplies
I'm finding it's harder to apply
Myself To my job
I got what I got
And I guess I Forget
That's what I wanted, never wanted alot
And I guess my soul still keeps my alive, barely
Wish I could say I Moved on, rarely
Am I thinking of you, is it temporary?
Or am I destined to be shriveled and weary?
Maybe the truth is to far down

In this mess, which I found
Between the blood and fury, I Found
Myself, the iceberg, miles down
In the glacial Seas, as the sky turns light brown
Like this turkey in front of me, forcing myself to eat
Friends giving, Cause what else do I have but defeat?
Family doesn't Want me
But then again, I need
To feel some sort of family
Can't escape this feeling, so lonely
I still question, How are you so happy?
And I guess, it's unsatisfactory
The place my mind leads me
And how, this could just be
I'm going down, the ships sinking with me
And I'm covered in twilight, breathe
But I can't seem to freeze
Or somewhat receive
This overwhelming belief
That I am not enough, I am not me
Just a former husk
Just a shadow, crawling in dusk
Onto the walls, this husk

Inhabited and punished by bad luck
And everyone asks me how I have been
Like they could understand how I have been
And that's why I write this in the bathroom, where have I beenm?
Between screaming and crying, from what I've seen
You fill indifferent still, I guess thats what I should expect
I guess I shouldn't pay you the time and respect
I guess I hate the feeling of this prospect
Buried beneath the surface, Deeper, I was A project
And I can't see with my eye, save me the hysteria
Bury it down, but I can't survive, listeria
Infecting me, back and forth, manic hysteria
Pay me the Favor, Let me move forward, blooming wisteria
Still dancing to the pounding drum
Still Drunk of the rum
Back to the fact
That I am still a bum
And I hide that, I choke it down
But between this pain and anger, I found
A middle ground

Between this season, which drown
The very earth, in its engraved trenches
As if to serve as liquid Benches
A series of kelp and icebergs, sticking up like wrenches
But hey, void of illusion, still pulling me, pinches
Just wrap me close to the bottom of this iceberg
Cause there's no going around, i have to continue forward
And if I don't, then forever, I'll move backwards
The tidal waves, echoing my craving
This suffering, absent yet your still creating
Maybe I've buried myself to far down
Never to surface, never to be found
And between these Glacial walls, my friends watch
A two way mirror, grimes, never washed
My brain, melting into slush
Grappling with the emotional cost
Of cutting you off, I scoff
But I know I'm better off
Actually, am I?
Cause there's still A void in my eyes
Did I not realize
The cost of Cutting you out of my life

But I never fully cut you out
I just say that, but that's not what its about
I didn't actually cast you out
I just forced myself To be alone on this route
It's not a matter that you left, you never left
You just submerged deeper, And in this theft
My hearts missing, and the deeper this iceberg goes
The more pelting of cascading snow
I find myself forever in your show
I thought I cut you off, but the taste of you is leaving slow
With each painful second, extending into minutes
Dividing the Hours into dividends and fractions
Is this the cost of my assertive actions
And your Replacing, an aggressive reaction
My friends keep knocking on the door, incessant
I'm feeling- I don't know, obsessive?
Maybe I was a little to possessive
Maybe I need to talk to my counselor, respectively
I just Wish I could understand your perspective
You left, but I'm still in your directive
I kicked you out, Now lifes been hectic

All these emotional swings, to and fro
All these phases, swinging fast yet slow
And I am so ready to run and just go
Into the sunny horizon, Buy the sun dies in the collapsing snow
This iceberg, forever menacing
My soil pays the foul penalty
For not wanting to repair what we had
And now, I sleep in the same pad
That we once shared
The burden, I now bare
Has built up, are you even there?
Or just dissociated from reality, crippling from the fear
All my friends say I need To macleat clear
Am I moving forward or stuck staring at the rear
And I'm taking the time to debate with this existence
I guess you really where my weakness
Pale to stale prison
Guess I'm still ignoring the lesson
This tidal wave, crashes upon me
Debating and waiting, crumbling Me
I guess I'm too far gone to be freed

To be something more than what is me, that what I lead
I'm still coming To the terms of the deed
That I signed and sealed, but didn't read
The fine print, in which, I, suffocate
Between Choking and screen, perforated
Tear open and proliferate
The way we dance, innate
Like this sorrow and me are prison mates
Fear of you, it complicates
My very life, and to see you with such happy strides
And it was childish not to See, the zebra disguise
To mistake the lions man for stripes
I let the lion into my life
And now I pay for that very life
Your gone, but the taste Ahead
Still feeling like one of lovecraft's creatures
Misunderstood in my depressing features
It's just sad, to know what Once was
And what once could have been
I'm just barely keeping it together, like I was
When we were Together on the scene
And like the titanic, I'll sink before I reach shore
I'll sink, before I reach the tunnels core

Escaping the Light, forevermore
And I'll keep my Void of a heart, locked behind a door
like love is a currency, used in a store
Your just another thief
Dispersing this stress of grief
For something I swore to keep brief
I just can't seem to keep
My pyrite word
Playing like it is gold's worth
Unsheathed my wooden sword
Roses rotting, darkening the world
I lost Myself in losing you
That much has proven itself true
And now as I grapple, with this iceberg so blue
And what was once a win, I now rue
Who would have known, it was impossible
Yet somehow, still probable
Between sorrow and thankful
I can never grapple
With the reality of my situation
Here's the translation
These feelings, subverting confusion
Cause I can't escape these emotions
And I guess, I wanted you to show remorse

And I guess, I wanted you to get off your horse
And I guess, even in your absence, you left a curse
And I guess, this is more than a hearse
And now I'm laughing as I write this, it's funny
All these moods wings, lonely
Now I feel ready
To move on, forever lonely
But in that, I gotta be a straight up guy
the Previous five lines where a lie
And I'll Just be orbiting your life
Passing you, never nearby
All this superstition, placating your fiction
I guess I'm like water, needing the path of least resistance
Why am I entertaining such Hesitance?
Just drowning In my stubbornness
How can you just forget my existence
When you have become the difference
My kryptonic weakness
But still, nonetheless
I need to move on, nonetheless
And if tonight I die
Would you remember my
Struggle and triumph

Was I ever enough
Throw me away with the rest of the stuff
You keep buried under those scales, shields up
I'm sinking in front of this iceberg
Never moving forward

To
Leah Johnson

Ice Breaker

Breaking Through, Mickeal Hip

I dream, through phosphorus lights
Swinging, left hook to a right
And as I stare into the absence of light
I have come to terms with this minority
It took me hiding in a bathroom
To finally come to
Admit, The elephant in the room
And is there nowhere left to go?
Rock bottom of this show
Is this what I am always destined to know
Well, I finally have the courage to say no
I'm a fire, flickering among the sea
Of this cavern, Similar to me
Your Exhausted, dissipating
And you Left me anticipating
For everything more, so sharpen my teeth
Travel Far beyond the reef
Take me back to sleep

Take me back, that's what I need
To relive, to receive
Some sort of relief
A reason to actually believe
Well, dangling like cold cuts
Take my medication when I wake up
This worlds a meat freezer, I'm frozen
But finally, warming up
In the eyes Of gaia, the mother
Returning Calls to its senders
I'm alright, never been better
Despite this Tumultuous weather
And I was gasoline, your the spark
The flame, ablaze in my heart
My eyes, just a optical part
I take my mark
Sharpen my teeth, it's warfare
Cause neither
Of us can't stay here
But I already know, your above here
And I guess this all goes to show
That we do not Know
What we gave, until push comes to shove
And the figment of our love absolves
And We can't keep it alive

Unless We choose it with pride
You've had your teeth in me, for far to long
And I'm done composing this song
I don't know why it took me this long
But this burden, I will not longer prolong
Grow back your claws
And to the raven caws
I'll ascend above newton's laws
Freeing myself from the maw
The broken teeth of this jaw
Ascending, ascending, retreat in your Paws
I can peacefully fall asleep
Once again, because rest is what I need
And when I dream
Without you, I see a chance
Of becoming something serene
Like unloading this package
I keep with me in this evolving scene
And when I awake, I will undo the damage
And move past this Place, clean
The dirty, stained slate
And finally empty my plate
To begin anew, starting from this date
And onwards, To think it was once too late
But Now, not soon enough

Biting through these chains, I see I am enough
A paradigm shift that ends this wintery tough
Putting down the chains and the cuff
That kept me bound to this hollow place
Leaving, with A smile on my face
And your desire, your need to race
I'll keep up at my own place
Because I am enough as I am
Between the dagger in one hand
And the pen in the other hand
Surveying the grassland
I'll take a chunk of my shoulder
Before someone treats me colder
Done carrying this boulder
Consider this closure
I need everyone to see what I have become
To this wounds, I once, had succumb
And now, I have overcome
And hold the future in my palm
And in This moment of clarity
I guess it goes to show, the mentality
That you, were possibly
The worst form of modality
On my, once crimson soul
And all the strings you pull

I'm done selling my soul
To you, this contract, is null
And this love, that you didn't want around
Stay on the ground
As I have now found
My peace, above this stormy sea, I have found
My heaven, above the dirt And magma
Rejuvenating my stamina
Ridding myself of miasma
Poisoned By our back and forth
I finally capitation This sword
Your worth none of the time I can afford
With these ticking seconds, I move forth h
And when we met, it was no accident
And it set a harmful precedent
And now, as you dream to become some sort of president
I move forward, to the present tense
With the coming season
You gave me the Reasons
To Leave you with your treason
You were Always leaving
Ascending, transcending
All of this, rescinding
The sea, descending

Finally, never missing
To give into the fury of this crescendo
Everything comes to its metaphorical end
And this quid pro quo
Is a cycle, that will never begin
To never again, sink so low
With me, again
Even if I have to move slow
I'm am happy With this end
And as I take these memories and null
I let the next era begin
The stain of this epoch, lining the canvas
Locked in a box, crimson Stained canvas
Leaving that part of me on the college campus
Where you found me, leaving that abyss
Finally behind
To pay it no mind
To finally confine
My self, leaving this all behind
And this ghost of our love, once haunting
Forever looking and daunting
The accomplishments I inspired, your flaunting
Remember this mantra
Cause I need you to see me for what I am
Not a puppet you can play with in your hand

And even though you left me on this plot of land
Every decision, meticulously planned
Because spite was always your brand
And even you it's the stars you land
Atleast, in one hand
I will be happy, and satisfied To know
That I let this package go
And descend, ending this show
Finally leaving the oceans below
And going above
Soaring with the doves
Finally, accepting I am worthy of love
Something more, then that dark cove
You forced me to bathe in
The same noxious gas I breathe in
And you divide Into dividends
I have finally come to my senses
As if this statue, has Become sentient
I was once a recipient
This fall out, in the present
This cycle, malevolent
And along these blinding lights, to a pathway higher
And between these Weaving right, I obtain my power

My final, triumphant hour
And yourself, you will devout
Selling Yourself out, till there's nothing left
Stealing from others, blatant theft
I see you, I'm glad you left
So I can move on and let
My soul wander onwards
Forever moving, forwards
My battle scars shining as I ascend skywards
Your born of blood and swords
I'm born of words and fire
This, was Destined to transpire
Thanks to you, I inspire
To become akin to that fire
To spread my wings, like a phoenix
And take our past, leaving It
And between the poison you spit
And The bottom I Hit
I finally feel better, in mind and spirit
And maybe, now that I hear it
You know, that I don't fear it
It being the deadly phosphorus
That kept me in this space, blasphemous
I am the beast, missing puzzle piece, gnawing off the calice

Growing past this abyss
You had left me with
And for this stint
We move forward, I took the hint
And in motion, One last blink
And I cleanse myself under the sink
My triumphant song, in a wink
You'll miss me if you blink
Not that you ever needed me anyways
But now, those are past days
I move on, because the way
Illuminated, all of this in play
No self brought misery can bring me back to you
Leaving you in the ocean blue
That Much, Alone, is true
This fate, I choose
Because what is there left to lose?
Tis my desire
That stoked the surrounding fire
And now, sinking in your pyre
I watch the burning remnants of your empire
Finally, unfolding matrimony
Broken by my new found autonomy
Moving on, from this void so deadly
Past the void and the masked party

Finally, we can let down our defense
Standing on opposite fences
Is it, that you need to feel above
Cause you feel so below
Is that why you ensure the dove
And drain it of its blood?
Do you not like the reflection in the mirror?
Acting like it's muddy, painting it to make it clearer
Ruling everyone's life with a iron fist, a reaper
A selfish empower
I relinquish your chains, and still, I'll remain
Happy with What is associated with my name
And you'll go on, cheating at life's game
A lion roaring without a mane
Your not as scary as you appear
And as the Emotions disappear
I finally cut this reverie
Coming to terms with reality
The illusion of you has finally dissolved
And now, this can all resolve
This problem, now solved
Finally frees me of it all

To

Leah Johnson

Running It Back

From, Mickeal Hip

My mind's running laps on an open highway
A thick tar burning the light of day
And a finale act in this play
To move one and freely sway
This two way vision
From a final freeing decision
From a emotion of overwhelming confusion
And I pray to God, that I stick to this decision
And when you call me, I'll leave this behind
And not pay you a piece of mind
But yet, there's a voice that's behind
And it needs to confined
Are you autumn leaves?
Will you fall and forget me?
And did you ever believe?
That you were deserving of me
If nothing else, then say it
Is it the autumn leaves, or a spirit
That possessed you

That left you, hearing it
I obsessed over you
But now, the bough has broken through
This prison released me from you
Is it really you?
And you'll sail the ocean blue
Always finding Something to leave
An ancient canopy
The night sky, We laid beneath
This has all come back to me
I'm starting college again
Not giving up on my dreams
Justifying my means with the end
Between these ancient screens
I enter the halls
Standing tall
And, now that it is fall
I recall
Where we met, where wd entwined
And upon the cafe we dined
They smiled at me, all left behind
Your were never to be mine
But Still, I run it back
This thick tar and the illuminating stack
Of words I never said, everything I packed

That you would probably attack
I'm not going To lie, I want to send you a letter
To come to peace, and with the colder weather
There's an actual hope that I will be better
A parallel Reason for that letter
And I guess I just need to leave this now
And in a way, I know how
But I'm nurturing the sow
And do you still believe, that now
Nothing else but yourself matters
Will life, to you, always be a ladder
Something, Of which will never give laughter
But suck out all the pleasure
Well, let this ocean belong to you
Let this iceberg surround you
There's nothing left to do
But disregard you
And let this be true
That I didn't deserve you
That the ocean blue
Will stay within you
Within those cell like eyes
Behind the bars and the growing rye
I begin Anew, my
Fate finally lies

With me and my hand
Not that you would understand
And as I put the paper in my hand
I don't really care if you understand
"Uhm, dear Leah, I should have never
Let you get the better
And pull me with your weather
And I acknowledge that with this letter
I hope you found better
Are you still endlessly climbing ladders?
Something your doomed to do forever
And do you even remember me?
Under all the falling leaves
Do you still believe?
That ambition will give you the relief
That you so willing believe
That you forever need
And when you Sleep
Do you Still dream?
Do you still scream?
Do you still plausible that scene
To try to make something so serene
In your eyes, It's still winter
With the cacophonous weather
Like a pricked splinter

You'll bleed forever
Never satiated, Never happy
Because dreams are not reality
And in that formality
You may find some vitality
And between the white in your eyes
I still remember when they met mine
And we crossed that playful line
We will tangle endlessly, entwined
But for the last time
Understand, you will not be mine
I am no longer sublime
Give me the day, you can have the night
I do not want to continue this plight"
And now that the past Is burning
To the college, everythings returning
To some sort of normal, Proliferating
Some sort of hope, churning
Itself with the fate, that I am creating
A muse that will not be manipulating
Or taking What I have been granted
And duplicating
Some sort of fake personality
To distort my reality
Unlike you, I am happy to be me

Cause now I can see
That we are not alike
You are a knife
I am Pride
I do not need materialism to survive
And now, I'll walk in happy strides
And among these Ancient ceilings
Where you had planted my feelings
All the skin, peeling
I'm done kneeling
Again, the ocean belongs to you
So take that with your blue
I am someone new
Not that it was me you ever knew
Give me a couple of more minutes to mourne
This contagion, once airborne-
Now, I am reborn-
Immune to your scorn
Your poison, spreading like pollen
And how many times have you fallen?
Upon the blade you were holding
I'm done just stalking
This shadowed figure of you
Because that's not you
And I'm done feeling blue

Believing in something not true
And as I move forward
Balancing my rose and sword
You'll regress backwards
Never wanting to look inward
And see the person you Burned
The person you inferred
That could not return
So give it the time to churn
Cause I'm done thinking of you, every Second
Do you reckon?
That destiny bestowed this burden
That had made such a problem
And is it your coping system
To always ignore the question
The problem being how you see yourself
And never caring about anyone else
And once the rain gathers
Does nothing else matter?
But your self?
And Nothing else?
For once, I can stand to see me
For once, I want to be
For once, I Am happy
With this reality

This shuffling campus
Filled with students, countless
Who will never Know your existence
But I do, along with your weakness
Your pride, will bury you
But maybe that's You
The person you can't stand
Because you simply don't want to understand
What makes you... The person who stands
In the mirror
It'll never be clearer
Until you are done fearing her
Feeling finally divine
I unwind
And become myself Again
Finally, this cycle ends
And for the last time, I am mine
A blotch Of white in this blurring line
So now this ends...
Thank you for the lessons

To

Leah Johnson

Reflection

So we finally come to the end. Back where this journey had begin, and every begins anew. A blank page of which I will now be able to write on, to redefine who I am and what I stand for. To think that I could not stand the person in the mirror.

Once muddy, now clearer.

So what is the lesson I take from all this? That lesson is that I deserve better than I give myself credit for. That everything that happened wasn't my fault and never will be. That, although I may be to blame for dating her, that I am not the fault for the cold indifference that had crushed me like a boulder.

What I have learned is that I am deserving of love. That I am above what she treated me as. And even though, occasionally, I may get the emotion, which paralyzed me, it is not my fault. It is simply the way it happened.

In a way, I came to terms with the obsession, ending it's possession.

My hesitation may have had reason but that reason now moves on from what it once was. I now understand that I am a human being, and I deserve to be treated nothing less, but also, nothing more. Hopefully you can feel the same.

My infatuation went to show the things I had ignored. If I had put emotions aside and understood the notions presented In Front of me, I could have changed what happened.

But now I can't. And that's okay.

So, love yourself, as I love myself. And understand that you control your fate. You rise and fall depending on how you make the situation. Make your future yours. Be the person that you want to be.

Don't be a stoic statue. Be you.

And for me? I will continue being me. That is all I can do. Thank you.

About The Author

Andi Galupa is an author, Artist and musician. But all of her passions share the same need to tell a story, luckily, she has many means to express them through.

Being a trans-woman, she has been through alot in her life, giving her the experience to write the stories she does. Or to explore concepts that people usually won't look deeper into. That is her mission.

To understand the misunderstood.

Made in United States
North Haven, CT
24 September 2025

73077045R00187